notes from
the Internet
Apocalypse

notes from the Internet Apocalypse

Wayne Gladstone

Thomas Dunne Books
St. Martin's Press
New York

THOMAS DUNNE BOOKS.
An imprint of St. Martin's Press.

NOTES FROM THE INTERNET APOCALYPSE. Copyright © 2014 by Wayne Gladstone. All rights reserved. Printed in the United States of America. For information, address St. Martin's Press, 175 Fifth Avenue, New York, N.Y. 10010.

www.thomasdunnebooks.com
www.stmartins.com

Designed by Steven Seighman

The Library of Congress Cataloging-in-Publication Data is available upon request.

ISBN 978-1-250-04502-7 (hardcover)
ISBN 978-1-4668-4334-9 (e-book)

St. Martin's Press books may be purchased for educational, business, or promotional use. For information on bulk purchases, please contact Macmillan Corporate and Premium Sales Department at 1-800-221-7945, extension 5442, or write specialmarkets@macmillan.com.

First Edition: March 2014

10 9 8 7 6 5 4 3 2 1

For Romaya

notes from
the Internet
Apocalypse

1.

DAY 1. THE HAPPENING

When the great crash happened it was nothing like we feared. There was no panic. No tears. Mostly just slammed fists and swearing. The Internet was down, and hitting refresh didn't work. "Ctrl, alt, delete" was also useless. No one had Internet. Anywhere.

And we didn't know why. Electricity, running water, and even television were all unaffected. But Internet Explorer mocked us with an endless hourglass, and Firefox just kept suggesting an update that never came. Mac users were confident Safari would never fail them, but it did. Although, because the Internet was down, no one tweeted "UGH! Safari! FAIL!"

We went to sleep that night with no e-mails sent. No statuses updated. And millions of men all over the world checked that secret panel in their basement wall to see if their old Jenna Jameson DVDs were still there to play them to sleep. Tomorrow, we thought, would be a new day.

DAY 2. THE WAITING

Some woke at dawn. Not on purpose, but withdrawal can be a bitch. They were the first to see that nothing had changed. A few walked out bewildered into the rain. Others remembered that television still had things called weathermen, who advised them to take an umbrella on days like this. By 9:00 A.M., our mood was best characterized as one of bemused frustration with actual panic still an arm's-length away. Many offices canceled work. It was like getting a techno-logical snow day, and swapping the Internet for some time off seemed like a fair trade at the time.

Personally, I was in favor of anything that relieved me of my duties at the New York Workers' Compensa-tion Board. Seven years ago, I had overseen the turn-ing of our department into a fully paperless office. The thought of coming back to a desk flooded with photo-copies and interoffice memos delivered in scribble-scratched envelopes was too much to bear. Not just the work, but the return to a place that no longer showed any sign of my one accomplishment. My more recent (and last) attempt at greatness was met with less approval. I wrote a memo two years ago suggesting that the state could save millions in worker compensation payments if it delivered free and mandatory antidepressants to all its employees (including employees of the workers' compensation offices) to prevent all the disability claims stemming from crippling workplace-induced depression and, of course, botched suicide attempts.

"You realize this is your job, right, Gladstone?" Noonan asked, curling my memo in his hands. "It's not a place for your jokes, regardless of what you've got going on in your life."

I studied the comb marks in his polished gray hair, not fully understanding.

"It wasn't a joke," I answered, but it hadn't really been a question.

By then, no one asked me questions. Like when there had been a change in office policy about Internet use. An interoffice e-mail sent to all employees, but it might as well have been sent only to me with a cc to the others solely for shaming purposes. A reminder that the Internet was to be used only for work-based reasons. Certain websites I'd frequented had been blocked. Nothing wildly NSFW, but things that couldn't be justified either. Noonan dropped my suggestion on my desk and walked away.

So I was happy to stay home, and did so with a clear conscience, knowing that not everything was broken. After all, my Scotch had yet to suffer any technical difficulties. I poured myself two fingers of The Macallan, pleased with my alcohol-based observation, and considered using it to update my Facebook status before remembering that would be impossible.

DAY 7. TAKING NOTES

One week now and I'm trying to keep this journal on more of a daily basis. As real-time as life will allow. I like the writing. Without work and the Internet, I need something to keep me busy. I focus on the pen scratching paper. It directs my mind and steadies my pulse. I can express any idea I want without some Twitter character limit or fear of a "TL;DR" comment following. Still, I miss the tiny dose of fame that comes from being heard online, where comments are tethered to content people are already reading, and statuses appear instantly on your friends' screens. There's a comfort that comes from knowing people are already staring at the pond when you cast your pebble. Knowing there are witnesses to the ripple before it expands out into nothing. So I play a little game and pretend others will read this. That I have a story worth telling. Otherwise, I might as well go to the gym or do crossword puzzles until the Web comes back.

I should go grocery shopping, but I keep thinking FreshDirect is going to be up and running again.

DAY 8. THE ELECTRONICALLY UNASSISTED ORGASM

Some parts of society are adapting better than others. Most offices are back in session, relying on faxes, phone calls, and the realization that 50 percent of all e-mails never need to be sent. But while Corporate America is finding any way possible to crawl toward profitable quarters, social circles are still floundering. People are trying to remember how they got their essentials before the Internet. Specifically, sex. No more eHarmony or Match.com. No more Facebook creeping. You can't even flash your junk on Chatroulette if you want to. How are we to get our groove on in this new world?

I say "we" because it's easier to talk like that. To pretend this is a history. A contemporaneously recorded log valuable to sociologists researching the moment when the world went offline. But my perceptions come from news reports, not field research, and mostly I only assume the world is wondering about sex because I am. Dr. Gracchus said it was time to move on. To get out more. But after nearly ten years of marriage, I didn't know where to begin. So I stared at the nicotine stains on his fingers and nodded the way you nod to psychologists. They need the reassurance. But now, completely unplugged, I'm somehow even more unsure of what comes next than when I first tried to live alone.

Without a computer to put my options before me, I

searched my memory, finding only movies from childhood in its place. Where would Val Kilmer or Tom
Cruise go to get laid? Bars! And it turns out it's true.
You can find women there. But unlike the Internet,
these women are three dimensional (sort of) and when
they laugh, strange noises come out in spasms instead
of "LOL."

Last time I checked, there was still a bar a few
blocks from my apartment. I remember the loud
drunken frat boys and wannabe gangstas stumbling
outside years ago, looking for their cars at two in the
morning. Romaya and I, already in the full-blown
nesting mode of an early marriage, would awaken and
crawl from our futon toward the window in darkness.
Sometimes we'd wing pennies at their heads. Other
times we'd just shout "DUH!" and fall back to bed
while they looked for the invisible source of abuse. I
guess it was childish. Like Internet tough guys shaking
their fists in anonymity, but we thought it was funny.
Besides, I liked to pretend that in their drunken stu-
pors they believed it was the universe itself rejecting
their bad behavior. Maybe that's why it helped me
sleep. Also, it made Romaya laugh when moments
earlier she'd been angry. I was her hero.

I stood in front of my bedroom closet trying to figure out what to wear. Over time, my wardrobe had
apparently devolved into an uncomfortable association of business casual and '90s grunge. I was doubt-
ing my ability to score in Doc Martens and flannel
when I considered my old corduroy sports jacket cur-

rently hanging in the hall closet. I bought it at a college-town thrift store and wore it incessantly through senior year and the years that followed.

"People think you're a colossal douche for wearing that," Romaya had said one day, while we pretended to read books that mattered under an arts quad tree.

I had been running my fingers through her thick brown hair sprawling across my lap, and had asked, "Do you agree?"

"Yes, but I like when everyone thinks you're a douche," she'd said. "It means I get you all to myself."

I decided to go for a button-down shirt with rolled-up sleeves, jeans, and some brown Kenneth Coles Romaya had bought me several years ago when I guess she got tired of having me all to herself. I was pretty much dressing for invisibility.

There was nothing on the other side of the peep-hole, and I opened my apartment door, suddenly aware of its weight. Building codes required a steel door as a fire precaution. I rode the elevator alone down to the dull silent echo of the lobby. The mailboxes lined the wall, waiting in their polished brass, but the super had brought me my mail only this morning. I had a bad habit of forgetting about it until my little slot was filled, so many of my bills and communications happening online.

The air between the foyer's set of glass doors was motionless and dead, but I stopped and took a breath anyway before heading out into Brooklyn. Everything was just as I'd left it.

It was too early on a Thursday night for the Crazy Monk Saloon to be packed. I was greeted by several anonymous faces that didn't look too different from those I'd abandoned a decade earlier. But they were different. They belonged to people who were too young to have moved into the successes and failures of their lives. My face had seen both, and there was no comfort in coming home.

I cut directly for the bar, securing a Yuengling before carrying it to my private stool at a high-top table for two. The bar continued to fill and I found comfort in the wall as I took stock of my surroundings, looking for journal fodder. Reality was troubling and new. Not just to me, but to my fellow patrons who struggled to look attractive in real life.

There was an energy I hadn't felt for a long time in my fingers and forearms, and not a good one. It made a tapping I didn't want to make, and movements were quicker than intended. I checked my watch and threw glances at the door, pretending I was waiting for someone. After a few minutes, something brushed against my leg. I looked down and saw a quite attractive, but somewhat overweight, woman. Her makeup was flawless, her chin and jawline were perfectly defined, and her ample cleavage was lovingly showcased as I looked down at her and she up at me.

She had lost a contact, but I kind of felt she lingered on the floor longer than needed in order to recreate a flattering Myspace or Facebook perspective: the extreme downward angle accentuating breasts while forcing a slimming perspective. It worked surprisingly well.

"Can I buy you a drink?" I asked, thinking people must still do that.

"Um, sure. Okay," she said, and settled into the perched stool. "My name's Donna."

"Nice to meet you, Donna," I said, noticing her agitation. "Is something wrong?"

"No, um, it's just this stool," she said, feeling around and hoping to adjust its height like an office chair.

"Tell you what," I said. "Why don't you settle in and I'll get you . . . a beer?"

"Michelob Ultra, please," she said, resting her chin on the table.

"Sure thing."

I returned to the bar fully aware I'd have to order something masculine to balance out the embarrassment of the Ultra. I scanned the Scotches and whiskeys along the top shelf, looking for a cost-effective option, and that's when I noticed the reflection of a muscular man in a ridiculously tight shirt. He was using his phone to snap pics in the bar mirror while flexing. I ordered my Jameson and Ultra while he tapped the woman next to him.

"Check it out," he said, showing her the phone. "When the Internet comes back, I'm gonna make this my profile pic."

"Cool," she said, or appeared to. It was hard to hear her clearly through her pursed duck lips.

I headed back to Donna, a drink in each hand, but as soon as I turned, I was confronted by a startlingly beautiful eye. I'm sure there was a body connected to it, but all I could see was a vibrant blue iris speckled with green. Perfectly maintained lashes framed the brilliance, and the colors radiated out along the curling black lines. I pulled back to adjust my perspective, allowing the second eye to come into view, and when I took a further step I saw those brilliant eyes belonged to a face that contained no other attributes nearly as appealing. Not unattractive, but clearly she was accentuating the positive. Of course, I can't really be sure because just at the moment I got enough distance to let the lines of her face form a picture, she darted up to me again—lids ablazin'—going eyeball to eyeball.

"Hi," she said, "I'm Samantha," and took another step until my back was firmly against the bar.

"I'd shake your hand, Sam," I said, "but mine are a little full."

She was too close for me to drink comfortably, which was too bad because, if my memory of early '90s beer-goggling t-shirts and baseball hats was correct, it would have really helped her chances.

"Well, it was a pleasure, Samantha, but I have a friend waiting for me," I said, holding up the Ultra, and heading back to Donna who, I noticed, had swapped out her height-appropriate stool for a chair that barely put her head above the table.

"Um, you sure you want to sit in that chair?"

"Oh, yeah. It's much more comfortable," Donna said. "Thank you."

"Well, maybe I could join you and sit in—"

"No!" she barked before recovering. "I mean, please, just sit down. I didn't get your name."

After years online, I'd gotten used to not giving strangers my real name. Even my Facebook profile had been created under just my last name to avoid the spying eyes of nosey employers. And without even thinking, I gave that as my identity.

"Gladstone," I said.

"Oh . . . is that your first name or last name?"

"Last."

"What's your first?"

"I'll tell you when I know you better," I said. "After all, maybe you're just some frustrated spammer running a phishing scheme in bars."

She laughed. Then she didn't. And then there was nothing.

"So . . . pretty crazy with the Internet, huh?" I offered.

"Yeah, totally."

We attended to our drinks. Occasionally, she'd adjust her breasts and look up at me in a still way.

"I hope it comes back, I have so many pics to upload. Wanna see?" she asked, offering her phone.

I flipped through about a dozen pics, all with her face at three-quarters and shot from above. She had it down to such a science that if you printed them out and put them in a flip book, it would create only the illusion of a pretty-faced, moderately overweight woman standing still.

"So, did you come here alone?" she asked.

I thought of Tobey. I couldn't remember the last time I'd gone a week without speaking to him, and I missed his stupid IMs. What started as a mutual admiration over five years ago had blossomed into a beautiful friendship, or at least a beautiful acquaintanceship that lasted years while my real-life friends seemed to fall away over time. I was a faithful reader of his horribly inappropriate celebrity news blog, and he was a big fan of those three lists I once wrote for *McSweeney's*. We messaged nearly daily, but had almost never spoken, even on the phone. Still, I was confident he'd be a good wingman and wished he were here instead of L.A.

"My friend's meeting me," I said. "He's late."

I continued to scan the bar. Some people were fine, but we weren't the only ones having trouble talking. I noticed what appeared to be a couple at the bar. Or at least a man and woman standing somewhat near each other in silence. After some deliberation, he leaned over and overtly "poked" her. To my surprise, she blushed for a moment, giggled something to her girlfriend, and then firmly pressed one outstretched finger into his shoulder. They stared at each other for a moment, and then left the bar in unison. Whether it was to have sex or just say dirty things to each other from across the room while mutually masturbating is difficult to say.

"So, how ya doin' on that drink?" I asked. "Can I get you another?" Her beer had hardly been touched, but I noticed I'd apparently killed my Jameson.

"No, I'm okay," she said, "but if you need another . . . what was that you were drinking?"

"Oh, I guess it was Scotch."

"Really," she said. "Seemed like Jameson."

"Yeah."

"But that's Irish whiskey."

"Yeah."

But this wasn't the Internet. Her eyes required more of an explanation than an empty chat box.

"I guess I call it Scotch," I said, "because that's what I want it to be. Sure I can't get you another beer?"

She just shook her head without speaking.

"Okay. BRB. I mean, be right back, heh."

I got up and headed to the bar, hoping more alcohol would lubricate my way through this awkward dance, but as I got farther from our table I realized I was also getter closer to the door. Two more steps and I would be through it, and then I'd be headed home where the Scotch was already paid for, and I didn't have to remember to smile for fear the natural curve of my mouth would be mistaken for anger.

I made it through and kept walking at a steady clip. I felt bad for Donna, but I wasn't worried about running into her again. That was my last time at the Crazy Monk Saloon. Nothing about the night felt right, and even the streets were strange to me. Like one of the rusty wires in a bundle of threads holding Brooklyn together had given way, adding an unseen tension to the rest. More fractures were coming. I needed to get back inside before it reached critical mass and snapped with the fury of a dragon's tail, knocking down buildings and severing limbs with its flailing.

I kept my gaze fixed on the front entrance of my building and walked as fast as I could. And even though my focus was directed home, I couldn't help noticing something wrong about the way a group of guys were forming a circle around something across the street. I shut the lobby door behind me, almost silencing the sounds of a cat being made to do things it didn't want to do.

2.

DAY 21. ACCEPTANCE, ZOMBIES, AND TOBEY

Three weeks now. We know it's not coming back. Clergymen, sociologists, and other really boring people take to the airwaves to talk about the return of a simpler time. A time of truer human connection. They think losing the Internet is like leaving your favorite sweater on a train. It's not. And while it might be overdramatic to compare it to the removal of an internal organ, it's certainly fair to say the Internet had fused with our body chemistry. Information and instant messages came and went with a rhythm as constant and involuntary as breathing.

Dr. Gracchus had told me that losing a spouse could cause a period of extreme disorientation. That two people's minds join after a time, each handling certain tasks for mutual benefit. And I guess it's a bit like that. But the point is, the talking heads are wrong. The loss won't bring back a simpler time. Only a search for something new to fill the void.

Romaya used to look for reminders of Northern California in Central Park. Especially if it were a wet day when the rain hung in the air instead of falling. She'd stare up at the leaves and branches, remembering the redwoods where she searched for Ewoks as a girl. Then she'd scratch at my scruff and tell me I smelled like a teddy bear. I was the home she had found. If I knew she were coming, I once told her, I never would have wasted all that time with people who weren't her.

"Me too," she said, running her hands around me. "It would have been nice to know I had a friend waiting in New York."

I know what was going on in that circle the other week. I've seen the bands of shuffling Internet junkies aimlessly roaming the streets from my window. Wide, sad eyes seeking out any trace of what they have lost. They devour anything they think can provide the fix they crave. The media calls them zombies because zombies are aimless and hungry and because the media is bad at its job.

But I've seen enough to know I'm better off inside. It's all over TV. After years of getting entertainment and information online, television feels strange. The commercials. The lack of interaction. It's big and bright, and even the more somber and sophisticated programming carries the brash 1980s taint of neon and synth. Like trading your iPod in for a jukebox. It's only good for destroying the silence.

Not everyone has fallen into zombiehood, of course. The world goes on. People find a way. But enough. Enough former members of society who will just never be right. After a time, the like-minded form circles. Different Internet rings meant to re-create the experiences of their favorite lost websites. Sexually frustrated libertarians meet up with one another, and soon they are entwined in a Digg circle. Each participant takes a turn in the center, sharing the latest news he has heard. Sometimes, it's something about a government conspiracy. Other times it's just some terrible cartoon they've found. The data is scrutinized instantly by the group who, if sufficiently displeased, will bury the bearer. There are conflicting reports about what that means. Most say it's just an expression, but some disagree, and the bands do keep seeking new locations in a ravenous search for more news and members.

The zombies I saw last week were part of a YouTube circle. Without a replay button or a link to similar entertainment, they demand hours and hours of mindless joy from whatever is unfortunate enough to be trapped inside their view. So many innocent cats have been worked to death, forced to do tricks for zombie-amusement without food, water, or chance of escape.

Although I hadn't heard any reports about Internet zombies breaking into people's apartments (or even looking at people who didn't remind them of the Internet), I decided to board up my windows. Just felt right. I didn't get very far, because at no time in the last ten years did it occur to me to stock my apartment with stacks of plywood. I contemplated the seemingly bizarre availability of substantial amounts of finished lumber in zombie movies and wondered if I could order some by phone. I'd need to go downstairs and ask the super.

The dead bolt snapped back with a force that echoed on the other side of my fire-prevention door. The door chain came next, but I didn't turn the handle, which struck me as odd because I was positive I wanted to. That's when I heard a knock.

It was Tobey. Bloody, sweating, and out of breath, but still Tobey. You could tell by his No One Is Ugly After Six Beers baseball hat—worn ironically, of course.

"Can I come in?" he asked after entering.

"Tobey? What happened . . . and why aren't you in L.A.?"

This was only the second time I'd spoken to Tobey in person. The other time was on a business trip to a Risk Management seminar in L.A. I'd crashed at his apartment and we stayed up until 3:00 A.M., drinking and playing Six Degrees of Stanley Tucci. (Bacon was too easy.) But other than that inexplicably entertaining night, ours had remained an online relationship. And more specifically, an instant message relationship. Even those IM exchanges were punctuated by long unexplained pauses, which I assumed were caused by the responsibilities of his online job. But apparently that had nothing to do with it because even in real life, Tobey left my question about what he was doing here unanswered, and headed off to the kitchen.

"What's going on?" I said, trailing behind.

"The Internet, Gladstone. Haven't you heard?"

"Yeah, of course I've heard, but why are you in my apartment?"

"Because," he said, holding the nearly empty bottle of Yuengling against his bruised cheek, "someone still has it."

"What?"

"It's true. I heard it in a Reddit circle just outside your apartment. How do you think I got these bruises? Man, those dudes did not like my defense of Corporate America."

I was slow to respond, and not just because Tobey was now eating from my jar of peanut butter, assisted only by his finger, but because nothing about this made sense. Online, Tobey was a name. A green dot. A series of sarcastic, meta-humorous messages that broke the monotony of my day. But in my kitchen, he was a twenty-nine-year-old man-child who blinked a little too often and moved with more energy than was required to accomplish any task.

"Tobey, seriously. Sit the fuck down. You're getting me nuts."

Tobey pulled a chair from the kitchen table and sat down. I handed him a napkin and another beer.

"Are you hurt?" I asked, but then I got distracted by another question. "What do zombies do in a Reddit circle anyway?"

"Mostly talk about how much Digg circles suck," Tobey said. "But occasionally, you hear a good rumor. Even zombified Redditors know their conspiracies."

"And you heard someone in New York still has the Internet? How?"

"How do you think, G-Sauce? They stole it."

"What does that even mean? It's not the Pink Panther diamond, it's, I don't know, it's the Internet."

"Hey, I'm just telling you what I heard. You don't like it, take it up with the zombie Redditors, but I don't know. It just feels right."

"It does?"

Tobey moved with the ease of a man without a job. His limbs conserved no energy for reports to be written. His mind eagerly soaked up anything in the ether without fear of losing more important details. It was a freedom that made him so light he couldn't even sit still in his chair. He went over to the sink, washing his bruises and stains before drying off on the towel hanging from my stove. Then he put his hands on my shoulders and looked me straight in the eye. Even as a grown-up, he still had a few freckles dotted across the bridge of his nose.

"The Internet lives, Gladstone," he said with a smile. "And it's here. In New York."

Suddenly a vague disconnect bubbled up the way it used to when I'd detect a fraudulent claim at the bureau. Little things you'd think people wouldn't bother to try. Blaming a preexisting left arm injury on a right arm incident. Or sustaining injuries in a workplace ladder fall and presenting with day-old black-and-blue bruising only minutes later.

"Wait a second," I said. "You only just heard this rumor. But you were already in New York. Why?"

Tobey picked at the decal of his Mr. Bubble t-shirt. "Well, y'know, the site's been down three weeks. I got nothing coming in. . . ."

"I don't follow."

"Well, I was down to my last thousand bucks."

"So you used it to come here and live off me? Why not save it or use it to pay your bills until you get a new job?"

"What bills? I do all my banking online."

"They'll just send them to your home."

"But see, that's the beauty of the plan. I don't live there anymore. I'm off the grid, baby!"

Off the grid. The phrase caught me more than I expected, and Tobey could tell he was on to something.

"Let's find the Internet, Gladstone. Someone's got it."

"It's not so easy, Tobes. Unlike you, I don't just crack jokes online. I have a real job to think about."

Tobey took a step closer. "First of all," he said, "I resent the implication that making up funny one-liners about how fat Jennifer Love Hewitt has gotten is not a real job. But more important, are you serious? Being a desk jockey for the Workers' Compensation Board? That's a real job? Judging from the amount of beer in your fridge and the fact that you're wearing jeans on a Tuesday, I'm guessing you haven't been there for a while."

"I'm working remotely," I lied.

"Working remotely or not even remotely working?" He smiled.

"Wow. That's a good one."

Tobey really was the best two-paragraph blogger there ever was.

"I know. I just wrote that. And now it makes no sense because there's no Internet." He paused for a moment. "Also," he said, "considering there's no Internet, that was the worst lie ever."

I wasn't sure why I was fighting Tobey. After Romaya, and maybe even before, my life had devolved into a fluorescent haze of desktop Outlook/Internet Explorer/Excel screens by day followed by laptop Chrome/Facebook/Netflix nights. Two equally useless existences separated only by the F train.

"Holy shit, I was gone for two minutes," Romaya had said, probably having pissed on yet another pregnancy test, "and you're back on that fucking laptop. You're gonna turn into some sort of cyborg."

"I was just Googling fertility stuff," I'd said.

"Right."

"Seriously, I saw something about more pregnancies going to term when the mom gives lots and lots of blowjobs."

"Do they have to be you?"

"Of course not. I'll just watch you service the whole third floor. I mean, how else am I gonna get an erection?"

She had laughed, but she hadn't wanted to. "Y'know, you take every important or hard thing in your life and turn it into a dirty joke. You know that, right?"

There was nothing keeping me. And in the back of my mind, I remembered Dr. Gracchus owed me a favor for clearing a certain questionable workplace injury in his office. It wouldn't be hard to have him verify my depression-based disability and get me out of that office. But it was something else that Tobey said that really sealed the deal.

"It's a whole new world, Gladstone. We can be anything we want to be."

I was standing in front of the hallway closet now, remembering the things I'd need.

"What's the weather like outside?" I asked.

"I don't know. May? It's May out."

I wiped some dust from the handle and opened the door. Hanging there was my tan corduroy sports jacket from years ago. On the shelf above was a flask Romaya had bought me for our first anniversary and my grandfather's fedora hat from the forties. I took them all.

"Okay, Tobes. I'm ready."

"You're not serious. A fedora? You'll look like one

of those insufferable Williamsburg hipster douchebags."

"Says the guy with a chain on his wallet containing no money. Fuck you. This was my grandfather's.
And what do I care? It's not like someone's gonna take
a picture of me and put it up on FAIL Blog."

"Ooh, speaking of that! I got something for this
journey." Tobey reached into his backpack and pulled
out one of those Polaroid cameras from my childhood.
"To document the trip. Who needs the Internet, huh?"

"Tobes, y'know, you don't actually need the Internet to take pictures, right? Digital cameras still work
and download directly to computers and, y'know . . ."

But he wasn't paying attention. "What's in your
pocket?" he asked. "Your jacket's puffy."

I reached inside, removing my flask. "You mean
this?"

"I guess . . ."

"Let me fill it, and then we can go."

3.

DAY 22. RUMORS

On the second day of our investigation, we left the apartment early. I was determined this not be another day wasted, like yesterday afternoon when Tobey and I gathered nothing but rumors. We had taken the F train into the city to look for the Internet, and the only thing stupider than writing that was actually doing it. Tobey said we should start at Washington Square Park because he heard there was good intelligence to be had, but it turned out he just wanted to score some weed. Poor thing. My offers of flask whiskey weren't cutting it. Not surprisingly, the loss of the Net had little effect on weed dealings, and after a handshake, Tobey was on his way. So we walked around and talked and eavesdropped and mostly just made asses of ourselves while Tobey floated on his skank bud and I sipped too frequently from my flask.

Most of the day was spent debating trivia. What year certain movies came out. Who starred in sitcoms from our childhood. And each dispute ended with "agree to disagree" or "I'm telling you, I'm positive" or "shut up, you're such a fucking idiot." But without Google or IMDB at our fingertips, nothing was resolved. Nevertheless, Tobey can fuck off because Jason Bateman totally played the bad kid in *Silver Spoons*.

We got tired around dinner time and went back to my apartment. Not exactly the *On the Road* experience I'd been hoping for.

"Not exactly the *On the Road* experience I was hoping for," I shouted to Tobey from my bedroom before passing out.

"Is that a movie?" he called from the couch.

"A book! Jack Kerouac."

There was a pause. Then: "Christ, how old are you?"

Despite our early start, today wasn't looking much better. Some people were claiming the government had shut off the Internet to stop the groundswell of free speech and democracy. I didn't find that particularly compelling in a world where the Right was already kicking ass and taking names in the online public influence wars.

"Who said it was the Right?" Tobey asked.

That was a good point, and I pondered it while taking swigs of Scotch and wandering Manhattan. I suppose the Left was equally capable of such things, if such things were even possible, but I couldn't see liberals living without the Net. We love Daily Kos and viral videos too much. And you can't hoard the Internet like Gollum and his precious ring. Cutting the Internet off from the suppliers of content made it useless for entertainment and information purposes, leaving it mainly as a communications tool.

"That's pretty smart," Tobey said, exhaling a cloud of weed.

"This isn't L.A., Tobes. You can't just go all Rasta in the middle of New York."

"You gonna narc me out, G-man?"

I stopped walking and waited for Tobes to stop too.

"Was that an abbreviation for Government man or Gladstone?"

"Not sure. Really high," Tobey said, holding in his smoke.

"Anyway, yeah, that's not bad," I said. "I'll make a note about the communications thing."

It wasn't hard to find more conspiracies. A bunch of people were laying blame on Corporate America—specifically, "fucking Corporate America, man." But none of the rhetoric was particularly compelling because, let's face it, "the Man sucks" will only get you so far. Still, it was the most popular refrain as we went from parks to bars to coffee shops.

"Are you keeping track of suspects?" Tobey asked. "Write down 'Corporate America.' "

"I'm not writing down 'Corporate America' until

someone actually articulates a theory. People are throwing that phrase around like some racial slur. As if it held some talismanic power to create liability without proof."

This time it was Tobey who broke stride.

"Yes?" I asked.

"You understand that I'm, like, really high, right?"

"I'll keep it simple. You find me someone who can actually explain why 'Corporate America' would steal the Internet, and I'll put them in my journal as a suspect."

"Deal," Tobey said. "To Starbucks!"

"Is that a big Reddit hangout now?"

"Maybe, but I need like six espressos if we're gonna do this. I'm pretty much tripping balls right now."

We hit the Starbucks in Union Square in the hopes of sobering up, but that's also where we met Sean. He was a self-proclaimed Redditor, but clearly not yet zombified. Just agitated and holed up with a grande and stacks of papers. He must have opened the place, because he'd managed to score the corner cushy couch for one. His tiny table was filled with mountains of notebooks stuffed with highlighted clippings. I bet he would have rocked the microfiche back in the day.

I asked Tobey to stand back as I approached, considering that between the two of us, I was the one not wearing a t-shirt for the failed start-up vaginalbloodfart.com. (I can't remember what Tobes had planned for content, but he never made it past the t-shirt phase anyway.)

"Sorry to disturb you. Can I sit down for a second?" I asked.

"What?" Sean barked in a hyperdriven voice that shook like the loose flap of a car ashtray. "I didn't do anything wrong."

"Um . . . I'm not here to arrest you or anything," I said. "I just wanted to ask your opinion on some stuff."

I'm not sure if he fully believed me, but no one from Reddit can resist giving an opinion.

"Sure," he said. "Just be careful of my shit." He gestured to his papers.

"You thought I was a cop?"

"Yeah, or, I don't know, an agent or private eye, maybe."

"The fedora and sports jacket?"

"Yeah, I guess I just assumed that's what you were. Either that or some sort of hipster douchebag."

"Fair enough," I said, taking a seat. "I'm Gladstone. Mind if my buddy, Tobey, joins us?" I said, gesturing over my shoulder.

"No problem. I'm Sean."

Tobey flashed me the "one second" finger from over at the Starbucks fixins bar while he poured his coffee into the counter hole, making room for half and half and far too much vanilla powder.

"Apparently, my buddy is unavoidably detained, but I was wondering if you had any theories about the world going offline."

"The Internet Apocalypse?" he asked.

"Is that what we're calling it now?"

"Well, I am."

"Hmm, too bad there's no Internet," I said, stirring my coffee. "You could have staked your claim."

"First!"

"Exactly."

"So Sean," I said after infusing my body with caffeine. "Whaddya got?"

"Well, it's obvious, isn't it?"

"Is it?"

"Yeah, fuckin' Corporate America, man."

I was disappointed. All that information consumed just to muster a cliché. I'm sure it showed. Fortunately, that was only motivating to Sean.

"C'mon, man. They've showed their hand, or have you forgotten about SOPA? Their draconian little bill failed, and now they're still hemorrhaging millions in piracy. Without the Internet, we'll have to go back to buying CDs and movies. Think of all that revenue they stand to gain."

"Yeah, capitalists like money, but . . ."

"But nothing. That bill was going through in Obama's White House. Not some random neo-con administration. And it took the people, the Web, to stop it. But take away the Web, and well, what's left?"

I was impressed. Not by the sentiment so much, but by his ability to spew it in under five hundred words. No small achievement for a Redditor. Sean was pleased too, swigging hard on his soy latte (I'm assuming).

"That's a fair point, Sean," I said, "but Corporate

America is more than just one thing. What about all the investors and businessmen who've turned a profit off the Internet? Service providers, websites, and digital media. You think all those businessmen will sit still and let the entertainment industry cut into their profits?"

Sean thought for a moment, stacking and restacking his newspapers. I looked over at Tobey, who had struck up a conversation with some kid sporting those nauseating earring plugs. I was on my own.

"Well, I'm not sure, but all that means is there's some angle we're not seeing."

"Would that angle also explain how they'd even do that? It's not like the Internet's their own personal light switch."

"Maybe it is. After all, Corporate America has always liked to own things before they destroy them."

Sean went on to explain about how the car companies bought up all the stock in trolley cars until they had the power to dismantle them, thereby forcing everyone to get a car. When Comcast merged with NBC in 2010, that was just the start of the Internet resting in the control of fewer hands. It just got worse until it only took a small cabal to shut it down.

"Fair enough," I said, and wrote down "Corporate America" in my journal.

Of course, there was only one problem with Sean's theory: it was stupid. Capitalists like to play with their toys and there was no compelling reason I could see for them to take their ball and go home. Not this ball that was wanted by millions willing to pay for it. I explained this all to Sean, who continued to stare at his data while sipping coffee. After a moment, he wiped the foam from his goatee and said, "Well, fuck. I don't know. Terrorists then, maybe?"

DAY 23. OZ

It was a beautiful day. The kind that makes most people happy, but ultimately depresses me when I realize something as superficial as the weather can affect my mood. Still, the sun was shining, and I wanted to look at pretty things, so we set our course for Central Park.

I used to gawk at the sheer size of it on a subway map and be amazed that no developers had disturbed its pristine beauty. No industrialist had insisted upon access to the millions and millions of dollars of wasted prime real estate. But the truth behind the park is far more difficult to comprehend. Central Park is not a square of God's beauty so majestic that it pushed back man's skyscrapers by a sheer force of nature. Central Park is man-made.

Before the Civil War, it was just overgrown, sporadically populated land, but those inhabitants were displaced by Government decree to make way for Frederick Law Olmsted and Calvert Vaux's creation. (They won a contest.) There was a belief that if you forced all races and social classes to live among and literally on top of each other, under constant metro-politan pressure, then there had to be a release valve in the center of that social experiment. So men built not only fountains and bridges, but lakes and foliage. And when it was done, New Yorkers stood back and stared at something unique and free which belonged equally to everyone. A place used by celebrities and vagrants alike to see and be seen. Central Park was the closest thing they had to the Internet.

I hadn't been to the park in a long time, but, at first, it seemed unchanged. The trees and landmarks were all there, as were the joggers and the stoners playing Hacky Sack. But a harder look at the circles revealed some were filled with Internet zombies, and a few of those joggers were just the terrified people fleeing them. I was a little surprised. Even I was get-ting used to zombies. In another week, they'll be just like pop-up ads with the X hidden on the left side. You adjust. Learn a new way to delete.

Harder to ignore, however, are the Twatters. Clever, huh? That's what we're calling Twitter addicts now. Losing the Internet has forced them to interact ver-bally instead of microblogging their lives, but a lot of them still talk in Tweets:

"Ugh! I'm standing in line at the post office."

"I'm not eating the crusts on my sandwich because apparently I'm five."

"Oh, my god, the barista didn't leave room for milk, like some sort of ax murderer."

But not all the changes are so ominous or annoying.

As we sat and regrouped, I pointed out to Tobey that some of the park chess tables had been converted to Scrabble boards to meet the word addictions fueled by Facebook apps.

"Hmm, I didn't think folks would go for that in real life," I said. "Keeping score's a drag."

"I wonder if people will start farming again," Tobey pondered.

We sat there a little longer, but neither Tobey's jokes nor sips from my flask could quell my rising anxiety. Keeping this journal causes tension as much as it calms it. The writing busies my hands and occupies my mind, but there's something about the pen scratching against the thick textured paper that makes my words take on an uncomfortable weight. Online, words flow almost as quickly as thoughts without revision or purpose, the way they do when you're alone or with someone who's fallen in love with you.

This was the first time I'd gone to the park without Romaya or failed to visit the Bethesda Fountain, which Romaya called the most romantic place in the world. She made that decision on her own one day, not knowing just how iconic the angel fountain was. It just struck a chord with her.

"Tobey," I said, while unscrewing my flask for dramatic emphasis, "we're not doing this right."

"I don't know. Knees bent, ass planted . . . I'd say we're sitting on this bench like champs."

Much like a 2:00 A.M. text from a drunken acquaintance, I decided to ignore Tobey's joke completely.

"No, I mean, we're looking for information. But we're not getting involved enough."

"Gladstone, I'm not hitting another Digg or Reddit circle. I can't take it."

"No, we need to go deeper. Not self-styled Internet reporters and editorialists. We need to get behind the scenes. Hackers. What we need is . . ." I now took the swig of Scotch, really nailing the timing. "4Chan."

"You've got to be kidding me. You want to seek out a bunch of /b/tard hacking imps? Online, they gave us Rickrolls and LOLcats. Who knows what they're capable of in real life?"

"I'm guessing nothing," I said. "They did that behind the cover of anonymity. In person, I'm guessing we'll find Ken Kesey's Merry Pranksters, except inexplicably bitter."

"Don't disrespect the /b/tards," someone said. And upon closer inspection, that someone appeared to be a woman. And Australian.

Sitting on the neighboring bench in her boots, torn fishnets, and miniskirt was a living hyperbole of retarded sexuality. The pink streak in her hair, the heavy eye makeup, and the harlequin nails alternating in red and black all reeked of desperate Hot Topic posturing that spoke in equal parts to fourteen-year-old boys and dirty old men.

I took a moment before speaking, conscious that this was one of those dramatic opening lines that required a clever and witty response.

"Fuck, you're hot," Tobey said.

"Ignore my friend," I apologized. "Sometimes he forgets public spaces are different from chat rooms."

"I'm familiar with that phenomenon. So, you boys looking for the Internet? Because I could use some help in that area."

"We're all about helping you in your area," Tobey said.

"Zing." She sighed. Tobey tried a new tack.

"We're doing some heavy-duty investigative shit," he said. "We hear someone in New York's got it."

"Yeah, I heard that too."

"That rumor's going around Australia?" I asked.

"No, I got it from a Reddit circle in Brooklyn."

"But then why were you already in New York?"

"For fuck's sake. Because it's New York. You try living in Perth without Internet."

Her name was Oz, which was apparently short for Ozzygrrl69. Our newfound friend was twenty-four years old and made her living letting men watch her shower for money. Much like Tobey, the death of the Internet meant the loss of her livelihood, as we learned while exchanging introductions all the way around.

"So you came to New York to get your job back?" I asked, more than a little incredulous.

"Well," she said, "that and I'm looking for a friend."

Tobey's energy was palpable as it surged toward what he thought was an offer of companionship.

"Not a friend in general, fuckwit," she snapped before laughing. "God, that would be embarrassing.

'Uh, hi guys. Will you be my friend? I'm looking for a friend.' "

Tobey put his energy away.

"No, I mean, when the Internet went dead, I lost touch with a lot of people I knew."

"You're right," Tobey said. "Hopping a plane because you have no real-life friends in your home country sounds much less lame."

I dissolved the tension with a question. "All your Internet buddies are in New York?"

"Not all," Oz said, pulling another cigarette. "Just one, actually. I think. If he's still here. He started pulling away even before the Net went down."

I watched her smoke, liking the way she held her Marlboro Red too much. The purple lipstick stains on the filter were impossibly distracting.

"Not to be offensive," I said after bumming a smoke, "but you seem far too sharp to spend your time being a webcam girl."

"I have to shower anyway. Why not get paid?"

It was hard to argue with that logic.

"Besides, what's more degrading? Being seen naked or having a boss?"

I raised my flask. "To showering for profit."

"See that, Gladstone?" Tobey said. "Oz here has a perfectly legit reason for being a dirty cyber hooker."

"Oh, excuse me, sir," Oz said. "I didn't realize making fart jokes online was God's work."

"Well, it beats a real job."

Oz had to agree. "Fuck, yes. Seriously, Gladstone, how do you do it?"

"Well, I'd prefer not to," I said. "Actually, I've been preferring not to so much that I'm out on disability."

That made Oz very happy, and she took the flask from my pocket. I felt her nails graze against my chest.

"Cheers, daddy-o," she said with a hearty swig. "I knew you were too together not to be batshit. It's always the straight-laced customers who get their freak on."

Tobey laughed. "Daddy-o. See, Gladstone? You gotta change that outfit."

Oz shook her head. "Nah, it's kinda exhilarating to see someone dress like a douchebag in earnest," she said. "Too much irony these days."

"You look too young to know anything other than 'these days,'" I said. "You think things used to be different?"

"Christ, I hope so."

We sat there a little while, the three of us, smoking and drinking, letting the park pass in front of us like a full-scale IMAX screening, and it was nice. There was a level of comfort that should not have been and we didn't feel the need to ruin it with acknowledgment. In time, our talk came back to what started it: seeking help from 4Chan.

"Seriously, Gladstone. Have you ever even been to the /b/ boards on 4Chan? These are not people you want to know in real life."

"No, Tobes, I haven't. I don't even pretend to understand the connection or the difference between 4Chan, the /b/tards on its forum, and Anonymous. But I know something out of that mess smoked the cyber counterintelligence agency that tried to bring down WikiLeaks. And that's the kind of mojo we need now. Not loudmouths from Digg and Reddit."

"So say we all," Oz said, nodding her head.

"Was that a *Battlestar Galactica* reference?" Tobey asked.

"Yarp."

Tobey and I tried to conceal our intense nerd arousal.

"Anyway, you're both right," she said. "I would have sought them out already, but they're not the kind of people you want to be alone with."

I didn't blame her. Overt sexuality without the distance and anonymity of the Internet was dangerous. She stamped out her cigarette, but even when she was done, she kept her head down, as if inspecting the significance of the crushed filter on the ground. She was waiting for something. Something I would have realized instantly if it hadn't been so long since I'd spoken to a woman.

I remembered my first date with Romaya, if you could call it a date. Sitting on her dorm room bed listening to Nick Drake's *Pink Moon*. Me trying to find an opening. She looking too intently at the CD case.

I spoke one soft word and waited. "Hey."

Oz looked up with more innocence than I thought possible.

"Would you like to join us?" I asked.

"I guess I could do that, yeah. I mean, if it wouldn't put you out."

She looked to Tobey, who thankfully just nodded, although I would bet anything he was suppressing something like "Oh, cool, you'll put out?"

"Well, then, okay, gentlemen," she said.

I raised my flask in a toast. That's when I noticed the black ops helicopters. Troops and dogs emerged around the perimeter of the park. Some zombies approached the dogs, eager to see a stupid pet trick like they remembered from YouTube or take a pic so they could add a funny caption. They were summarily mauled. New York City, it seemed, was shutting down.

4.

DAY 23. LOCKDOWN

I wasn't positive what branch of the military I was looking at. Most wore black bulletproof vests over fatigues and had helmets not unlike Darth Vader's, minus the face piece and flare. Oh, and automatic weapons. There were a bunch of those. It reminded me of the days after 9/11 when soldiers were a welcomed sight. Their earnest posture and polished weaponry helping us believe we could only be hurt when our guard was down.

But, for some reason, these troops didn't bring that same assurance, even though the radios crackling in the park were reporting that the soldiers were a response to detected Internet activity in New York. Specifically, these intercepted transmissions all concerned terror-ist acts targeting Manhattan. So, as hard it was to be-lieve, it seemed someone did have the Internet.

"Radio, shmadio," Tobey said. "We'll see what 4Chan has to say about this."

"Major world governments are without Internet while some third-world enemy combatants have found a way to dismantle and exclusively harness its power?" I asked.

Oz stamped her cigarette out under her boot. "Hard to believe?"

"Yeah, but if it's true . . . well, it would be quite a tactical advantage."

"The Internet for communications purposes," Tobey said.

"Right."

We watched the troops establish borders and check-points around the park. And we watched the people watching the troops. None of it seemed real. The ex-perience was crying out for some hyperlink, carrying it to a validating source.

"So, assuming they let us leave eventually, how do we even find 4Chan?"

Tobey thought for a moment and then held up a Polaroid. "Well, about twenty minutes ago, I took this pic of a kid leading a blind man into a pile of dog crap. I bet he knows where to find 4Chan."

"You sat and watched a kid fuck with a blind guy?" Oz asked.

"Dude, you don't understand," Tobey protested.

"I haven't seen something like that in a really long time. It was like a YouTube video. "

Oz ignored the response. "Well, I heard 4Chan has been congregating in the Village."

"Why? Is there a NAMBLA support group there?"

Oz and Tobey didn't laugh.

"Dude, seriously. Not cool," Tobey said. "4Chan's no joke."

I looked to Oz.

"Playing with fire, Gladstone."

"Seriously? Man, I have got to meet these guys."

I made my way to the perimeter and Tobey and Oz followed. Bags were being sporadically searched, handheld metal detectors used. Occasionally, someone would be pulled out of line and questioned more extensively. There was even a screen set up for body cavity searches, if necessary. But all this hit-and-miss diligence made it impossible to predict what kind of terrorist plots they were hoping to thwart.

"Please step forward, sir," one soldier said, pulling me slightly from my companions. I complied.

He reminded me of a cop I'd met in college who made a similar request when he caught me posting fliers for my band. After checking my driver's license, he asked, "Don't you know there's a city ordinance against posting bills on public property?"

Oddly enough, that law had never come up in my Nineteenth-Century American Literature class.

"No?" I said, gesturing to the literally dozens of fliers already on the wall.

The cop stiffened reflexively, ready to smack down the punk in his way, before he realized I wasn't being a punk. It just wasn't logical to assume there was some law given all the posters flooding the wall.

"Well," he said eventually, "we don't catch everyone."

He let me off with a warning, but hearing the story later, my drummer was shocked I had been so compliant.

"Fuck, no way I give some cop my identification when I'm not doing anything."

"Well, apparently, I was doing something, and he wasn't a bully about it."

"Yeah, but why give him your driver's license before he even tells you what law you were breaking?"

"I don't know. Because he asked for it?"

It would be a few more years before I understood why I was friends with so many rebels but still didn't see things the same way. It had something to do with the difference between hating authority and hating the abuse of authority. And for the moment, these troops had not done anything to flip the switch that would blur the distinction between my drummer and me. I stepped forward.

"Where you headed to?" he asked.

"My apartment," I lied.

"To . . . ?"

"Masturbate? I haven't really thought that far yet."

"No, I mean, where. What address you heading *to*?"

Oz laughed in the way I hoped she would, and I wondered if I would have been as polite to that cop in college if I'd been under the scrutiny of a sexy neo-punk chick.

"I'm sorry, sir. My mistake," I said. "Brooklyn."

"That might be awhile, sir. You're free to leave the park, but for the time being, no one's leaving Manhattan. The subways and tunnels are closed. Now please move along."

I stood on the other side and watched dogs sniff around Tobey and Oz. Fortunately, Tobey had smoked the last of his weed about thirty minutes earlier, and after a few more questions, they joined me. Whether Oz managed to get free without a strip search was due to the soldier's professionalism or the repeal of "don't ask, don't tell" is difficult to say.

"So, how long you fags been conducting your investigation?" she asked as we started our journey.

I was a bit taken aback. "I'm sorry," I said. "Is 'fag' Aus slang for—"

"Dudes who fuck each other."

"Wow. Hardly politically correct."

Oz took a drag from her omnipresent cigarette before answering.

"I get naked for men on the Internet. How much political correctness were you expecting?"

Tobey laughed, but it made me a little sad. "What's your real name, Oz?" I asked.

Tobey broke the silence that followed. "So before

we throw ourselves into the lion's den of 4Chan, I was wondering . . . should we check in with Tumblr?"

"I've heard that word, Tobes, but let me assure you, I have no idea what Tumblr is."

"Really?"

"Yes, really."

"But it's for mid-thirties hipster douchebags like you."

"Also for fifteen-year-old virgin emo chicks posting their bad poetry," Oz added.

I looked at my two companions, waiting for each to disagree with the other's description.

"Oz is right," Tobey said.

Oz shrugged. "Yeah, I can't really disagree with Tobey either."

"Curious. You rarely see those two sharing the same shaded section of a Venn diagram. But even assuming Tumblrs are organized or forming zombie circles, why would you think they'd know anything?"

"Fuck, I don't know," Tobey said. "But I'm really having second thoughts about hanging with 4Chan."

We continued on toward the Village, and even when the conversation died, that was okay. We enjoyed the sound of one another's footsteps. The feeling of not being alone. Besides, we'd reached the point where people can't become any closer without disclosing painfully personal details or bonding over a shared traumatic event, and I wasn't ready to do that. Bring on 4Chan.

4Chan Unplugged

I observed something interesting: New Yorkers are much more helpful to provocatively dressed twenty-four-year-old Australian girls than they are to men over thirty dressed in crumpled sports jackets and reeking of Scotch. That might not be enough for a sociology paper, but it was a notable fact nonetheless. We met a fourteen-year-old boy who was using a skateboard and a staircase handrail concurrently for the sole purpose of destroying his testicles. According to him, the Bowery Poetry Club had been having a 4Chan members-only night every Thursday since the Internet crashed. That information was also confirmed by a fifty-two-year-old tattoo artist missing an eyebrow.

By a bit of luck or a one-in-seven chance, today was Thursday. We arrived at the Bowery Club around 8:00 P.M. and were greeted by a doorman with a clipboard and a white plastic bag wrapped around his head with holes for his eyes and mouth. Even in real life, 4Chan was retaining anonymity.

"What can I do for you, noob?" he asked.

"We'd like to come in," I replied.

He flipped the pages in his clipboard. "Well, let's see . . . you don't seem to be on the homosezwhat?"

"What?" I asked.

"EXACTLY!" he shouted, and high-fived another bag-headed man in the doorway.

I was going to reprimand him for the grade school

prank, but he wouldn't have heard me over Tobey's laughter.

"So," he said. "You sure you want to step inside? This is 4Chan. Not for the faint of heart. Especially to outsiders."

"Do your worst, /b/tard," Oz said, and stepped inside.

For a moment, I considered if it was her familiarity with the 4Chan lingo from the /b/ forum that got her through the door, but ultimately decided it had more to do with the fishnets. I dropped the cover for us and we followed. It was hard to believe we had gotten anywhere before she showed up.

"One sec," the bag-head said. "Let me get your change."

"Keep it," I replied over my shoulder, and kept walking.

The club was a standard bar in front with a stage and performing space in back. Small tables scattered the floor, and about thirty people, all with bags or masks on their heads, socialized in small cliques. It was like *Eyes Wide Shut*, but without all the money, prestige, and hot sex. So yeah, I guess it was just people wearing masks, about half of which were Guy Fawkes.

We made our way toward a table while several /b/ tards shouted, "Tits or GTFO." While I pondered why someone would verbally abbreviate "get the fuck out" when that phrase is composed of four one-syllable words, a waitress came to take our order. She worked for the club, and wore no mask. Oz ordered a vodka tonic, I asked for Jameson on the rocks, and Tobey cleared his throat.

"I'll have a Stella and your phone number," he said.

"Yes to Stella. No to number. So, Stella, vodka tonic, and Jameson rocks? Party on. I'll be right back"

"Seriously, Tobes?"

He was unapologetic. "This is a new world. We can be whoever we want to be. You've decided to be a film noir poseur; I'm gonna be a highly confident ladies' man."

"Wait a second," Oz said. "I thought it was the Internet that let you be a new person?"

"Does it? If I went on a date with that girl, she'd check out my Facebook page, she'd see who my friends are, what kind of parties I do or don't go to. What my favorite shows and movies are. She'd see my favorite quotation of all time is 'Narp,' from *Hot Fuzz*. She'd see it all. But now, there's nothing to call me on my lies. We're free of the inventory of ourselves. For all she knows, I'm a Los Angeles venture capitalist, accustomed to dating Filipino supermodels."

"I know that would be my first guess," I said.

The waitress returned with our drinks. They contained novelty plastic ice cubes with flies in them.

"Really?" I asked.

"Sorry," she said. "They make me do that. It's part of our rental agreement with 4Chan."

We all shook our heads and sighed, and I hung my

sports jacket over the back of my chair. Within moments a /b/tard swiped it and my hat. He jumped on the stage, wearing my clothes, giggling uncontrollably while screaming, "Look at me! Identity theft!"

I hadn't been in a fist fight since I was fourteen, and by an amazing coincidence no one had stolen my jacket since then either. I knocked backed my Jameson and then stood on my chair.

"Attention all 4Chan douchebags!"

The room fell silent, some with surprise, others quieted by their instant calculations of how best to hurt and humiliate me. I did not pause longer than I needed to. This was the Internet. Unless I fell off the chair and made grape-stomping lady gurgling sounds, their attention wouldn't last much longer.

"What happened to you?" I asked. "Yes, you. You were the agent provocateur of the Internet. The best and the brightest. True, some of you were functionally retarded and/or pedophiles, but think of all you've achieved. Internet meme after Internet meme. Legendary practical jokes and Anonymous's hacking abilities. Attacks on Corporate America and Scientology. The beating you gave to HBGary. A force to be reckoned with. A defense against government abuse. And that's not just me saying that. Didn't Christopher Hitchens call the 4Chan community lunatic and juvenile, but also alarming and brilliant?"

"No," someone shouted from the back. "We just said he did on our Wikipedia page."

"Well, that's still something," I said. "Look, I can't bear to see you reduced to this. Juvenile gags and practical jokes."

Now I had them. I could even afford to take a dramatic pause, and I did. And even though someone made a fart noise under their armpit, they were all still listening.

"My name's Gladstone. I'm looking for the Internet. Will you help me?"

The one who'd stolen my clothes jumped to the middle of the stage, mocking, "Ooh, look at me! I'm Gladstone and I'm looking for the Internet!"

Suddenly a loud full voice came from behind the stage curtain: "Silence, Sergeant Turd!" The curtain parted, revealing a man at stage right with a long velvet robe and a Guy Fawkes mask fancier than the others. All he had to do was hold out his arm, and the other 4Chan member quickly turned over my hat and coat. He was clearly /b/tard royalty.

"You raise a fair point, Gladstone. The Internet Apocalypse has been hard on 4Chan, depriving us of what we do best. But even now, we are not without our power and influence. And who are you to be so arrogant and stiff-necked before us? Personally, I thought those three *McSweeney's* lists of yours were a little too on the nose."

"You read those?"

"The Internet has put forth neither text nor image unseen by me."

"Forgive me, sir," I said. "I meant no disrespect. Can you help me? Are the rumors true?"

"Gladstone, I'd like you to come with me."

I stared down at Tobey and Oz.

"Are you coming, Mr. Gladstone?"

"Just me?"

"Who else?" he said, and disappeared backstage.

"Follow him," Oz said.

Tobey agreed. "Yeah, but watch your cornhole, bro."

I followed the robed figure into what I guess amounted to the club's green room. My eyes settled on the crumbs in the corner, moved by a quiet disappointment. I'm not sure why I was expecting a worldly study of leather-bound books, especially considering 4Chan just rented this place once a week. Nevertheless, the man sat on the unspeakably stained couch with such solemn dignity and offered me a folding chair so graciously it almost made up for the surroundings. I put my hat and jacket back on before sitting. I didn't want to be the only one without a disguise.

"You have some questions for me, Gladstone?"

"Are these rumors about intercepted Internet communications and terrorist threats true?"

"We believe they are," he said. "We have detected similar activity."

"Doesn't that mean you have Internet?"

"No, but we have the ability to detect a Wi-Fi signal and other markers. Doesn't mean we can get online."

"Doesn't it? I'm sorry, I was an English major. . . ."

"Then stop asking computer science questions. What do you really want to know?"

He leaned over to the side of the couch and, to temper his severity, handed me one of several Buds chilling in a bucket of ice. Not the choice of the elite, but sometimes a perfectly chilled mediocre beer is the finest beverage there is.

"Tell me, Gladstone. Do you visit our site often?"

"I think I can honestly say I've never been to your site. All my information is secondhand. The memes you've popularized. Your association with Anonymous. Your hatred of Scientology. Your alleged electronic haven for pedophiles . . ."

I could see his eyes tighten even through the mask. "Lies. 4Chan is a democratic nation. Think about it, Gladstone. What's the oldest trick for discrediting enemies? Kiddie porn. Sexual deviance. Those slanders are perpetuated by those who would marginalize us. But we are not the monsters the media has created."

Suddenly, a noise came from the closet in the corner of the room. He raised a finger to his Guy Fawkes lips. "Could be a raid," he whispered, and headed for the closet door. He slowly turned the handle and, in one sudden and disquieting motion, a naked fat man wearing a cheap Nixon mask fell wanking to the floor, hentai porn prints crumpled in his sticky hands.

"Glendoria4! How many times? This room is off-limits! Get out!"

The man stumbled to his feet, bowing and backing out of the room at the same time. "Sorry. So sorry, sir."

The robed man shut the closet door, keeping his back to me for an extra moment. Even through the heavy drape of his velvet, I could tell he was taking a deep quick breath to gather himself, before doing a quick military turn and settling back into comfort.

"I apologize for that disturbance."

"Not at all. I believe you were explaining how 4Chan isn't just a bunch of sexual deviants. . . ."

"I may have misspoken. But 4Chan has an open door. You have to let everyone in if you want to create a home for expert hackers, government informants, CEOs with predilections for sodomizing squid. It doesn't matter. We cast a wide net and some of the best and brightest call us home."

"And why do you guys have nicknames? I thought the /b/forums were anonymous."

"Yes, but real life changes things," he said. "We still keep real identities secret, but look around, you can't hang around a place like this and just keep addressing people as 'you' and 'that guy.'"

He returned to his seat and crossed his legs beneath the robe. "Now, let's return to your questions."

I killed my beer. He handed me another.

"These intercepted signals," I said. "Where are they coming from? Can't you trace the source and get this thing going?"

"We don't know that yet. All we know is that it's

coming from far downtown or maybe Staten Island. Do with that information what you will."

He stood up from the couch.

"Do you have to go?" I asked. "Won't you join me in a drink?"

"I would," he said, "but I'm not much for drinking alcohol through a straw." He pointed to the tiny hole in the mouth of his mask.

"Well, then take it off. It would certainly help gain my trust."

"No, Mr. Gladstone. In the age of hyper technology and cookie crumbs, you can only trust a man in a mask. Everyone else has too much to lose."

"I'm not wearing a mask," I offered.

He shrugged in silence. Something prevented him from saying more. Then he gestured for me to leave.

"Wait—before I go. Why are you telling me all this? I thought that was, like, one of the rules or something. Don't talk about the /b/forums."

"First of all, that's just during raids, and second of all, the only people who get all butthurt about mentioning the /b/forums are newfags."

I'm sure I looked visibly uncomfortable.

"Oh, I forgot," he said. "You went to college in the nineties. Don't take offense. These are just words for the masses. Not even. It's the Internet-speak we aquire. In any event, I'm telling you this because you asked for help. And I trust you."

"Because I have nothing left to lose?"

"Godspeed, Gladstone."

I headed for the door, but before turning, I asked, "Are you Anonymous?"

He remained motionless for a moment, but then stood full and proud, his red velvet robe long and flowing.

"Gladstone," he said. "You may call me QuiffMonster42."

5.

DAY 27. POLITICS IN THE APOCALYPSE

Picking locks isn't like the movies. It's a two-hand job because locks only open under pressure. You can poke at the spring-loaded tumblers all day and they will snap and fire back to position as soon as you run your pick over them unless the other hand is keeping it tight. A tension wrench primed and ready to turn so the tumblers stay depressed. I didn't expect to learn that in law school, but it was more interesting than the rule against perpetuities, and Martin, a student from Oregon, was eager to teach.

He also instructed me in the basics of making burglar tools out of everyday objects. If you place pennies on your thumb and forefinger, you can bend a paper clip into a zig-zag pick. And if you snap the metal clip off one of those cool leaky pens I'm so partial to and then bend it into an L, it makes quite the serviceable tension wrench. It was important that these things be inconspicuous because, as we learned in Crim Law, the mere possession of burglar tools was a crime, and we were, y'know, studying to be lawyers and all.

I'd sit on the radiator in my Fordham dorm room for hours, learning how to work the window locks. In their bolted state, they pulled back only a few inches into the room, allowing a mere sliver of air to enter at the very top. A safety/suicide precaution that succeeded only in providing an incentive to sharpen my skills, because if you popped the lock along the bottom, and turned the handle sideways, the entire window opened like a door. Romaya loved that. Not only because it was wrong, but because it brought the stories that much closer.

That's what she called the people living in the luxury apartments across the way. Each in their own boxed reality and on display for us. Grown-ups. Some pulled the blinds, but others probably believed in the anonymity of New York. The privacy of living in the sky, surrounded by concrete. They were unaware two kids in their early twenties were committing a minor crime solely for the joy of sitting up in a darkened bed, smoking, and watching them live for our amusement.

There was a single man in his thirties who watched TV for four hours every night. An aging woman who did her face and hair endlessly, and another room that was impeccably furnished, lit, and exposed, but never occupied. No actor ever took the stage. But we watched anyway, content to witness the real world from the safety of youth. It couldn't find us there. Not in the dark. But just to be sure, we'd snuff the glow of our cigarettes and lock the window before going to sleep.

To my credit or shame, Oz feels safe sharing the bed with me. It helps that we keep something between us—her sleeping under both the sheet and comforter and me sandwiched between the two with only a sheer layer of cotton separating my broken desire from her body. The last few mornings, I woke first and had a few moments to watch the covers rise and fall with her breathing. I stare at the flush two blankets bring to her cheek and try to divine her dreams. But the peace Oz finds in her sleep makes her inscrutable.

We've been spending time downtown based on that crumb of Internet intelligence from Anonymous. It seems Occupy Wall Street's numbers are growing again. Almost as strong as when they made the world sit up and take notice of their constitutional right to take a dump in Zuccotti Park.

It was unseasonably cold this morning and we ducked into the white-tiled lobby of Deutsche Bank, looking for some coffee. Apparently, it had become OWS headquarters.

"Fuck me. Did someone wash a goat in a bucket of patchouli?" Oz said, holding her nose.

Tobey shook his head. "Smells like a pair of Birkenstocks took a shit in here."

Mostly college-aged kids, but some older folks, were milling about in clusters, clearly in regrouping mode. Each was talking about what was really going on, what it meant, and what they had to do. At first, I thought recent changes had revitalized their economic protest. Without competition from the Net, shop owners had been free to fan the flames of inflation. And while that might have been good news for those businesses, computer and gadget sales had tanked along with all the tech and marketing jobs that go with that. Firms and businesses kept laying off IT people too. After all, how many guys do you need to fix your Excel spreadsheet or document management program? But one look at their signs and I could see this was no longer about the economy: GIVE US BACK THE NET; YOU CAN TAKE THE WEB, BUT NOT OUR FREE SPEECH, and one of what I'm guessing was Che Guevara wearing a Guy Fawkes mask?

"Who are these signs addressing?" I asked. "The man? They're acting like they know who took the Net."

"Time to investigate," Tobey said. "I'll kneel down behind that white guy with the dreads. You push him over and we'll beat the truth out of him."

I had a better idea. There was a girl with big nerd glasses, striped stockings, and a purple bob.

"How about her?" I said, pointing.

Oz shook her head. "You really can't help yourself, can you?"

"Excuse me," I said, walking over to the girl. "I couldn't help but notice your sign."

She dropped a sandwich bag of what appeared to be weed at the sound of my voice.

"It's not mine!" she protested.

Tobey nearly pissed himself laughing.

"I don't care about your shwag," I said. "I wanted to ask you about your sign."

I pointed down to her posterboard, which read, GIVE IT BACK, to make it clear I wasn't talking about astrology. "Who exactly do you think took the Net?"

"Who do you think?" she said. "The government."

"Why would they do that?"

"Where ya been? Remember SOPA? The government's in cahoots with the entertainment industry. They want to shut down the Web. They shut down Megaupload and BTJunkie. Now they're like, fuck it, let's shut down the whole damn thing."

She kneeled to recover her stash, so I directed my question downward. "Obama wants to appease Hollywood so much he just flipped some gigantic kill switch?"

"Well, I don't know how he did it," she said, pushing her weed into her skirt pocket. "But yeah. Is that so hard to believe? Look how the government cracks down on us. Arresting us for sleeping on public property!"

"Well, Zuccotti Park was private property, and even if it weren't, I mean there are laws. If you were allowed to just set up camp everywhere we could solve the homeless problem in America by just passing out tents."

She looked at me with a kind of confused distrust. A touch of fear. Then she threw the weed out of her pocket again. "Why did I just pick that up? It's not mine!"

"Again, I'm not a cop. And I'm not even picking on your protest. I mean, it's good that there are laws. I mean, you *want* the cops to arrest you, right? Isn't that the point of civil disobedience? To get arrested for what you believe in? To prove a point?"

The look returned, but without fear this time. She retrieved her weed again and asked, "Who the fuck wants to get arrested?" before walking away.

"Smooth, G-Stone," Tobey said.

"I don't get it. If OWS thinks Washington took the Net, why are they protesting on Wall Street?"

Oz wasn't confused. "Because who wants to be stuck in D.C. without the Internet?"

She was right. I'd forgotten that while the exits had opened and people were free to leave, Manhattan's entrances remained closed as a security measure. Twenty-five percent of the city's population has now fled. And just like before the Apocalypse, all the most frightened and boring people took off for New Jersey.

That's why the three of us had decided to hole up

at Oz's hotel in the Village. Going back to Brooklyn would have locked us out of our chances of finding the Internet. I kicked in some money for Oz's room, and Tobey offered Oz his last fifty bucks to watch her shower. It's probably for the best she declined, considering I'm fairly certain he just wanted to make more lame Australia jokes. "Crikey, that's not a rack. Now *that's* a rack!"

"Well, what now?" I asked.

"Whaddya mean, what now?" Tobey barked. "We didn't even come down here for OWS, remember? We're following my dream."

"To be the most sexually retarded blogger the Net has ever seen?"

"Not that dream. The one I told you this morning."

Tobey claimed he'd woken from a vision: that we were well on our way to discovering who stole the Internet. I was skeptical and paid no attention. After all, most of Tobey's inspiring dreams involved jokes about how hot he still is for Demi Moore. ("If my right arm got sheared off in an industrial accident while Demi Moore was blowing me, my only concern would be losing consciousness before she finished.")

Furthermore, while I was clearly uncomfortable with the knee-jerk liberal OWS crowd, Tobey was also falling prey to the Right's growing influence. The Apocalypse had been hard on the political left. TV ratings and radio listenership were way up, and that's where the Right thrives. NPR is no match for the multipronged attack of Republican talk radio, and MSNBC can't compete with Fox. The Internet was the only thing that the Left was almost kind of good at. And while it's refreshing not to have my inbox flooded with sophomoric MoveOn.org vids comparing Sarah Palin to Hitler, it's a little frightening that even with a Democrat in office, the public influence war is over. All we have is *The New York Times,* and who's shelling out two bucks for a paper in this economy?

Tobey had got up from his couch, wiping sleep out of his eyes and holding court in the hotel room. "Gladstone," he said. "I've seen it. Why are we making this so hard? Terrorist Internet chatter intercepted somewhere downtown. Duh? Why don't we go to the Ground Zero mosque?"

"Park51? For the same reason we're not going to the Olive Garden in Times Square. It's a stupid idea. Plus, the mosque doesn't even come with bread sticks."

Tobey and I went back and forth until Oz threw off the covers to interrupt. "I know you guys think I'm just some chick from a country filled with crocodile hunters and baby-eating dingos, but if I could . . ."

"And Vegemite sandwiches," Tobey added.

"Yes. Vegemite sandwiches. Thank you. But it doesn't really matter who's right. We're out of ideas. Terrorist sympathizers or slandered Muslims, the mosque is downtown and we've got fuck-all intelligence so, y'know, why not?"

The Mosque Not at Ground Zero

The three of us left the OWS crowd and headed down Rector Street still carrying the supplies we'd gathered that morning. Like any mission composed of people who didn't know what they were doing, we decided the first thing we needed to do was pack. The Kmart in Penn Station gave us plenty of opportunities to fill our arms without reason. Swiss army knives, compasses, backpacks, and even a self-inflatable raft. It wasn't until we were done shopping that we realized our purchases were gleaned more from old *MacGyver* episodes than anything we might need in the Apocalypse. But seeing as we didn't know what that was exactly, who's to say they weren't the same thing. Besides, the whole *MacGyver* thing reminded me of Martin, and that made me happy. I liked remembering him from before he became a lawyer. Unlike me, he'd finished law school and settled in Alaska as a public defender. It didn't agree with him. He shot himself years later, sometime after we stopped acknowledging each other's birthdays even with the help of Facebook reminders.

I was surprised to find Park51 was still just occupying space in the abandoned Burlington Coat Factory while trying to raise construction money amid a sea of bad press. Tobey adopted a stealthy Spider-Man creep fifty yards from the destination.

"Ya think there's a way in through the roof?" he asked.

"No, but it has a front door, jackass. The center's open to all New Yorkers."

We walked into the spacious and inviting lobby. White walls reflecting all the sunlight that streamed in from the glass doors and walls of the center's lowest level. After a moment, we started gathering intelligence, which basically meant trying to walk around unnoticed while gawking for clues. Not the easiest thing to do for a punk Aussie, fedora-sporting Jew, and dick-joke idiot-savant Caucasian. Basically, we just kept moving. After a while we reached the gym, and Tobey soon found himself in a pick-up basketball game with three Egyptian exchange students from NYU. Then it was just Oz and me.

"Ooh, a Middle Eastern cooking class is about to start," she said, pulling a flier off a table.

"Z'oh my God! No way!"

"Fuck off. It sounds fun."

"Yes, Oz," I said. "It totally does, but we'll probably get more done if we split up. So why don't you hit the class and I'll check out the café area? We'll meet Tobes in the lobby in an hour or so."

"Suit yourself," she said. "But don't come crying to me when you're dying for my kick-ass baba ghanoush recipe."

"It's a promise."

I followed the familiar smells of caffeine all the way to the café. For all its Halal and Middle-Eastern influence, it wasn't too different from a Starbucks. Had the Wi-Fi been working, I'm sure there would have been more laptops in effect. And, as it were, there were still a few insufferable writers at work, presumably hacking away at high-concept comedies about Saudi Arabian princes forced to live with suburban Jewish families.

I got a coffee and started updating my journal while perched at a long stretch of counter two seats down from an Arab man, about my age, charting algorithms on a notepad while cross-referencing information in *The Wall Street Journal.* He wore an expensive and meticulously maintained white buttoned shirt with the sleeves rolled up. It looked like it fit him perfectly fifteen years or pounds ago. Now it hugged a bit too much, but he sat with such immaculate posture and moved with such purpose, it still bestowed a certain elegance. Occasionally, it seemed he might have been eyeing my journal and smiling. Not in a haughty way. Just quietly amused or maybe interested.

"May I ask," he said finally, "are you a writer?"

"No, not really."

He was disappointed, but unwilling to give up so quickly.

"But you are writing . . . ?"

"Well, sometimes I sing in the shower, too, but, y'know?"

A smile. "Ah. An analogy. Not so different from metaphor. Suitable for a writer. Or a lawyer, perhaps."

"I'm not quite either," I said, extending my hand. "Nice to meet you."

"Yes, pleasure," he said. "My name is Khalil. I'm visiting from Egypt."

"Gladstone. I'm visiting from Brooklyn."

My new friend and I got to talking. About his brief stay in the United States. during his early twenties. His return to Egypt to assist in his father's business. And how much New York had changed in his time away.

"There's a distrust I did not see sixteen years ago," he said. "Sure, I was a foreigner. A strange dark-skinned man with funny ways. Contempt, racism, even hatred. But there was no fear. Now I just don't understand."

"Well, you do understand, though, right?" I said. "It was no small thing that happened."

"Please. I apologize. I'm not minimizing 9/11. But had I stayed in New York, I could have very well been working in the Towers that day. I would have certainly been downtown. And now all Muslims are always the first against the wall. Like this foolishness with the Internet outage."

Okay. Now we were getting somewhere, I thought. Having an intelligent discussion with an honest-to-goodness Muslim right in the heart of the detected terrorist transmissions. Perhaps this exercise wasn't just an excuse to maintain a Scotch-based buzz while I roamed Manhattan.

"I don't disagree, Khalil, but given the detected transmissions, the animus of the Muslim world against America, and the history right here in New York, do you really have to be a bigot to be nervous about a solitary Muslim man crunching numbers five blocks from Ground Zero?"

A slow smile spread across Khalil's face. He was remembering someone, and it brought a happiness, especially now that the years had wrapped the memories in the comfort of wax paper. "You're a Jew," he said. "Yes?"

"Why so sure?" I asked.

"Only a Jew would be open-minded enough to come to a Muslim community center, while still opinionated enough to risk offending the people inside."

I sipped at my coffee and thought for a moment. "Well, if that's your definition of a Jew, then I kinda take that as a compliment, Khalil."

"Good," he said, and raised his spiced date-juice tea or whatever he was drinking.

"Oh, are we toasting?" I asked, removing my flask. "Well, as long as we're doing so much for international relations, maybe we should get the Scots involved." He offered his glass, and I spiked both our drinks.

"I wasn't sure if you drank . . ." I said.

"Yeah, I'm not too observant," Khalil said, taking a sip. Then he paused. "Did you say Scotch? This tastes like Jameson?"

"Yeah."

"But Jameson is Irish whiskey . . ."

"I know, but . . . I know."

"Anyway, Gladstone," he said. "Explain this to me. Some terrorists stole the Internet for their own purposes. Evil purposes?"

"That's the theory."

"So they can have old YouTube videos all to themselves?"

"I would think the greatest advantage of stealing the Internet would be maintaining all its communications power while depriving those advantages to your enemies. Also, Khalil, you're the one with *The Wall Street Journal* in front of you. Just the loss of the Net itself is helping tank our economy. Need there be more?"

"Economic terrorism. That's a bit more compelling."

"Yeah."

"But you don't really believe that, do you?"

"No," I said with a laugh. "Not even a little. But why don't you tell me why."

"Because," Khalil said, "America is at war with radical Muslim fundamentalists, not robots."

"Meaning?"

"Muslims like the Internet too. What terrorist group could win the hearts and minds of the Muslim people if it deprived them of Facebook and Twitter? Osama Bin Laden might have been holed up in an Abbottabad compound without the Internet, but his neighbor Tweeted the whole U.S. tactical assault. And how about the riots in Egypt when they took the Net away? That did not work out so well for the government."

Khalil had been dying to make this point, and I was happy not only to receive such a logical argument, but to have given him the chance to articulate it.

"I'm sold, Khalil," I said. "But tell me more about these robots."

Khalil hunched over with a laugh that creased the midsection of his lovely shirt. It was nice to end on a high note.

Tobey and Oz were already in the lobby when I arrived, and it was clear that after some time here even Tobey didn't believe Park51 was the hotbed of terrorist activity Glenn Beck had led him to believe. And even if it were, we hadn't found any trace of the Internet. We were about to grab our things and get wrecked at the Heartland Brewery when we heard it. Something I hadn't heard in at least ten years. An old-school modem with all its crackles and buzz.

"Fuck, I knew it!" Tobey said.

"Knew what?" I said.

"Don't tell me you didn't hear that modem. That's the sounds of the Internet."

"Yeah, I heard something, but why would anyone be using a dial-up modem now?"

"Dial-up?" Oz asked.

"Yeah, that's what that terrible crunching beeping noise is."

"I thought Chef Abdul was just mashing some more dates?"

"It's coming from outside," Tobey said.

We looked out through the glass of the lobby doors to see twenty soldiers in riot gear. The black stormtroopers from the park had returned. And that modem we'd heard appeared to be merely dispatcher crackles over walkie-talkies. But I didn't process that then. At that moment, all I could think of was the force of twenty troops plowing into the lobby, flowing like violence and filling it with screams for everyone to hit the floor.

Oz broke for a side door and was taken down instantly. I sprung forward as if the knee pressing into her back were actually driving mine, but a trooper blocked my way, screaming, "Get down! *Now!*"

Before I could even decide to comply, another guard screamed, "He's getting away!" I looked and saw Tobey slipping through the door that Oz had failed to reach before sprinting uptown with two troopers following after. They labored under the weight of their riot gear, but Tobey bounced off pedestrians all legs and elbows like an '80s video-game character.

I heard a familiar voice in protest. "What is the meaning of this?"

It was Khalil, standing right beside me and demanding an explanation from one of the troopers.

"Hit the floor. Now!"

"No, sir. I will not," Khalil said. "Under what authority do you come here and do this?"

It was a fair question, but not one the trooper was prepared to answer. It wasn't one he'd even thought to ask. He searched for an answer in his memory, in his training, but, ultimately, found it in the butt end of the rifle he jabbed into Khalil's face. Khalil dropped to his knees, pressing at the blood that flowed through his useless fingers onto the lobby floor and his pretty white shirt until the trooper restrained him from behind, cuffing him and laying him flat in the mess he'd made.

It felt like my moment. Greatness being thrown upon me by inequity. But that's only because I was looking through my eyes. In another instant, I was thrown to the floor just like everybody else. My own trooper for my back. My face inches from Oz. She looked at me, hoping for something I could not give, and I watched them drag her to the car outside and take her away. Her hand on the glass. Reaching for me or maybe waving good-bye.

Interrogation

Arrests weren't just something for other people, and narrating events into my journal didn't keep them from happening to me. After the raid, my journal and the things in my backpack were confiscated, along with my flask. I was placed in a van and taken to what seemed to be a conventional downtown office building. I didn't know why I was under arrest, or if I was under arrest, actually. Once sequestered, my cuffs were removed and I was asked to sit in a tiny conference room. The door wasn't locked, and when I poked my head outside, a woman at a cubicle politely requested that I sit back down. I looked at the exit sign over the stairs. There was nothing keeping me here.

"Please, sir. Have a seat. The agent will be with you in a minute. Can I get you some water?"

I closed the door on myself without a response and sat back down. After another twenty minutes a man in his early forties, devoid of body fat or whimsy, entered the room. He had my things.

"Mr. Gladstone," he said, pulling a chair from the small conference table between us. "My name is Agent Rowsdower. Do you mind if I have a seat?"

"Am I under arrest?"

Rowsdower sat and smiled. His teeth were too small or there were too many. Maybe both. Not sure. Something was wrong and less than human.

"Why? Have you done something wrong?" he asked.

"Good one. Where's Oz?"

Even a man with a deficient sense of humor would have quipped something about the Yellow Brick Road, but Rowsdower seemed to have removed any trace of the impractical by sheer force of will. He unzipped my backpack and tossed my journal on the table.

"Oz," he said with a smile. "Would that be the Australian webcam girl you write about?"

"What gives you the right to read my journal?"

"What gives me the right? What's the matter, Gladstone? Bright guy like you doesn't read the papers?"

"I used to get my news online."

"Right. Of course you did. HuffPo? Slate? Oh, probably something international for a less biased point of view. BBC. Al Jazeera, perhaps? Anyway, you might want to acquaint yourself with the NET Recovery Act."

He pulled my flask from the bag. "Here. Go ahead," he said. "You're not gonna like this."

I took a swig and felt the numbing warmth tingle to my arms while Rowsdower proceeded to tell me about the National Emergency Technical Recovery Act. Drafted by Obama's White House and passed by an overwhelming majority in both houses across party lines, the government had been granted additional state of emergency powers if used "in the direct furtherance" of restoring the Internet. This power allowed officials to interrogate and even detain "persons of interest" indefinitely without charges or representation by counsel.

"And how the hell did I become a person of interest?"

"Well, you tell me, Gladstone. Do you think in the last few days most New Yorkers have been consorting with Anonymous at covert 4Chan gatherings and visiting downtown mosques amid rumors of terrorist Internet chatter emanating from downtown?"

"Still doesn't make me a threat to national security."

"The government, not you, decides what makes you a threat."

I wasn't naïve. I'd worn a suit. Worked in an office. Voted in several elections. I knew the way the world worked and the dark things people accepted in silence. But Rowsdower was talking about them in a brightly lit room without a trace of shame. I must have looked very young to him.

"By the way, this Oz," he said. "You wouldn't happen to have her real name, would you?"

"No."

"Well, don't worry, Mr. Gladstone," he said, turning vaguely avuncular with his established power. "The government tends to believe you. I ran your background check. Law school dropout. New York Workers' Compensation employee out on psychiatric disability for the last two years. Not exactly the prime suspect for hijacking the world's technology."

"Two years? Check your stats. More like two weeks. No wonder Anonymous kicked ass in your counterintelligence wars. You guys are a mess."

Rowsdower remained calm. I was fairly certain everything he'd ever attained in life was gained from this ability not to react. To not say the things a more honest man would say. But there was something else at play I couldn't discern. Not quite empathy, but something. He took a breath.

"Am I correct, Mr. Gladstone, that you wouldn't want to talk to me about your wife, Romaya?"

I thought of Romaya in the hospital. An IV in her arm and red and wet eyes that dripped tears each time she blinked. Somehow, I got it in my head that pulling the IV could stop the tears, but I didn't do it. I just held her in the bed and placed my face against her wet cheek so she could hear me whisper, "I'm so glad I married you."

"Gladstone," Rowsdower repeated. "Am I right, you don't want to talk about your wife?"

"I'd prefer not to," I said.

"And why's that?"

"My wife is dead."

A pulse rippled across Rowsdower's face, beneath the skin.

"Right. That's what I thought," he said, zipping up my bag. "You're free to go, Mr. Gladstone. I'm sorry for the disturbance. I'll let you find your own way out."

"Out of a prison?" I asked.

"Prison? You must have noticed this is just an office building. Under the NET Recovery Act, the government is empowered to commandeer private property for the purposes of interrogation."

Rowsdower left the door open behind him. I was free to go, but I was alone.

6.

DAYS 29–31. DETOX

I stumbled out from the interrogation, searching for the closest landmark, but New York looked strange without my friends. And, of course, the world was still changing. Many businesses were closed and the streets were half-empty. Still, mailboxes overflowed with letters, and newsstands were overrun with porn. And not half-obscured brown-paper-bag-covered porn, but big stacking piles beside the gossip mags.

I hadn't bought a dirty magazine in over fifteen years, but I felt compelled to flip through a *Hustler* in front of a newsstand by Water and Wall Street. I remembered the feel of high gloss beneath my fingers and the smell of ugly maroon inserts reeking of colognes I'd never wear. But now the girls looked like girls. No longer the dark and dangerous sex creatures I'd hoped to meet as a man, but the kind of lost young women I wanted to save. And I felt bad because that didn't stop me from thinking of them exactly in the way I was supposed to. I put the magazine down and headed for the hotel.

Rowsdower had me thinking about Romaya. I held her behind the locked bathroom door, and tried to stay calm and strong while she hovered over the toilet and pissed on a pregnancy test. My law school suite-mates were oblivious in the living room, and on this side of the door we weren't discussing anything that didn't need to be discussed until we knew what two weeks late meant. I fidgeted in the shower, and then it was there: two blue lines against a background of white.

"That means pregnant, right?" she asked, checking the box.

We hadn't decided what to do. No point in making decisions without all the facts, but now there were facts.

"Marry me," I said.

"Shut up."

"Marry me."

"You want to marry me?"

"Since the night we got drunk and turned Clue into a drinking game."

"That was our second date."

"I love you."

I surprised even myself with how sure I was, but I was sure. Marrying Romaya felt right. It felt real. Law school was a delay from actual living. And if I kept going, in two more years I'd be a lawyer, and then what?

Tobey and Oz weren't at the hotel when I arrived. That didn't worry me at first. After all, Tobey probably didn't want to return to his last known address with agents after him. I was more concerned about Oz. What if she were still detained? Deported? I wanted to go back to the interrogation office, to Park51, to Central Park, to anywhere I'd ever seen her. But even with the population leaving in droves, this was still New York City. How do you find just one person? I sat on the bed drinking, and trying to think of a plan. Occasionally, I'd flip the pages of the *Hustler* I didn't remember buying and wonder why the twenty-first century seemed to prefer ass to the omnipresent tits of my youth.

And that's when I realized Rowsdower had drugged my Scotch. I couldn't think of a reason the government would do that, but I also couldn't believe I bought a porno mag without remembering it. Maybe they wanted to follow me. See if I led them to clues in my compromised state. Guide them to Tobey or the Internet. I didn't know. All I knew was that suddenly the room was too big, even when I pulled the covers and grabbed the pillows.

I've spent the last three days in my hotel room. Too anxious to write. Too anxious to do anything other than take comfort in the *Hustler* that speeds my heart and then slows it with release. There's a girl on page forty-two with a dolphin tattoo beside her absurdly coifed pubic hair who particularly excels at that. But then the fear returns, and I remember I still don't know where Tobey and Oz are or what to do without them. All I know is that if the government were hoping to find dirt on me in my altered state, they lost. For three days, it's been just me, the *Hustler,* and order-in food. Except once, I did leave to hit the corner liquor store for more Scotch. And even though the dude behind the counter asked if I was all right, I think the effects of the government's drugs have worn off by now. I think it's safe to look for Oz without compromising our operation. And even if it's not, I can't be alone any longer.

I figured if she were free, she'd be looking for work, and that would narrow the search, that is, unless she'd found that friend she was looking for, but I didn't know who that could be, and I couldn't think about that. I showered and shaved, but I still couldn't rid myself of the *Hustler* Drakkar Noir samples that had entered my pores by osmosis. I wasn't worried though. There were worse smells in Times Square.

DAY 31–37. PORN IN THE APOCALYPSE

When you manage worker compensation claims for over ten years, you start to know people. Which wounds can heal, and what breaks someone forever. I said from the beginning that losing the Net wouldn't mean returning to a simpler time. Shatter both of a man's kneecaps in an industrial accident, he won't take comfort in crawling. He'll undergo extensive surgeries, splints, physical therapy, and, ultimately, walk with crutches if that's the best he can manage.

And it's the same with porn. We need it back. But not the peep shows and smut peddlers of the '70s and '80s. We want all the ease, variety, and anonymity of the Internet. So sure, within weeks all the DVD and sex toy stores that Giuliani had pushed to Ninth Avenue in the '90s crept back to Times Square proper, but there was more. Capitalism has risen to the challenge of creating Internet porn in the real world, because drunken frat boys and men in raincoats will always buy movies and mags from smiling Pakistanis in brightly lit stores, but the real money to be made was in servicing the millions who indulged in the privacy of their homes.

In addition to the proliferation of standard porn stores, a surprising number of costume shops have popped up. Seemingly legit Halloween stores, but since this is June, it doesn't make sense. And though I was supposed to be looking for Oz, I had to investigate. I walked inside one on the corner of Forty-third and

Eighth and was struck by its size. There were a few anemic shelves with cheap masks, despite the handful of quality costumes that had been in the window. An Orthodox Jewish man purchased a pirate disguise, and then a business-casual dude bought a plastic Spider-Man mask held on by a stapled rubber band. But instead of exiting with their purchases, both men headed toward a back door. The Jewish guy removed his yarmulke with one hand while reaching for the door with the other. I followed.

"Sir, you need a mask?" an employee asked.

"I'm not sure."

I caught the door before it closed and ventured inside only to find a much bigger pornography store filled with men of all shapes and sizes. All wearing masks, and free to peruse the aisles without any fear of being seen or recognized. And if they'd been caught in the store's antechamber before purchasing their disguise? Well, the shops were still good enough for plausible deniability.

Other than that, though, the store was pretty standard. Movie aisles were separated by categories. Big circular antitheft mirrors hung in the corners next to surveillance cameras. Aside from the masks, the only other difference I noticed was the proliferation of fetish porn and the disproportionately high clusters of men in those aisles. Businesses were adapting. Anonymity was profitable, and the more I cruised, the more women I saw too. All in disguise. After a few hours and several visits to similar stores, I went home—without Oz, but with several cheap masks and a variety of porn I would never admit to purchasing in real life. I almost wrote that down as "IRL," but no need. This is the only life we know.

The morning came and the piles of magazines and DVDs didn't make my bed any smaller or quiet the razor as it roared across my stubble. I was conscious of my toothbrush. Even the corduroy of my sports jacket. Every sound of morning was deafening, clearly defined and unmuted by another body to soften the tin-can room. A tree that falls alone in the forest still makes a sound. It just wishes it didn't.

So as soon as I could leave, I fled to Times Square again. It was a good and loud distraction, and looking for Oz forced me to talk to people. I wish I could have Googled "NYC strip clubs" and "peep shows," but, instead, I just wandered the city following the smut and trying to avoid the Apocalypse's newest Internet zombies. Unlike the others who moved in circles re-creating their departed websites, these men roam the streets in file like a string of suddenly naked Rockettes, their flapping dicks as overt and nonsensical as their desire. Of course, I'm talking about the Chatroulette zombies. I could call them flashers, and I guess that's all they are, except I'm not sure they would have come to this if not for the Internet. The website was like a gateway drug to their perversity. But at this point, who am I to judge?

I keep pretending I'm making progress, but when the Scotch runs out, the panic fills its place. Without Romaya, without a job, without the Internet, or even my companions, I have become too aware of time. And too aware of my attempts to kill it by describing a post-punk Aussie to random smut peddlers and strip-club bouncers. No one has seen her, and I wonder if she's found a real job. A place to live. Her friend. But then why wouldn't she leave word at the hotel desk? Could I really just be forgotten, defriended, blocked like some random name on the Internet?

For the first time as a New Yorker, I'm accepting the things people are trying to hand me because I don't want to miss a lead. I gobble up the useless fliers being fed to me, but the barkers don't know the girls, and the bouncers think I'm a cop so they don't talk much. The girls talk, but only when you drop a twenty for a dance, and they're too used to telling men what they want to hear to be helpful.

In one place, a blue-haired girl named "Osiris" approached me for a dance. Cleopatra eye makeup, torn fishnets, and Doc Martens. Maybe buds with Oz. It was worth a shot at least.

I set my fifteen-dollar Scotch aside in safety and offered up my lap.

I instantly got a dirty look from the black stripper I'd rejected minutes earlier, and it made me feel racist, but I didn't have twenties for everyone, and I had to pick the girls I thought Oz would know. (That kind of makes Oz sound superracist.) In any event, Osiris turned her back, and bent to the floor so I could see what was about to be ground into me. Then she went to work.

"I'm looking for a girl," I said.

"Well, you found her."

"No, I don't mean like that."

My words were lost into the back of her head. She was sensing the pulse of the music with her outstretched arms while feeling for my rising erection with her ass. It was important to get proper alignment to facilitate the grind.

"What?" she asked.

"Could you turn around?"

She did a quick mental calculation. "Okay, but no touching."

"No touching."

She turned to straddle me, her thighs over mine.

"I'm looking for an Australian girl," I said.

"I can be Australian," she said in quite possibly the worst accent ever.

"No, you don't understand—"

She took my hat and placed it on her head. "Crikey! Wanna come to the champagne room with me, mate?"

"You want to be an actress, don't you?"

"I am an actress," she said defensively, then returned to character. "And a crocodile hunter! Whaddya say? Champagne room?"

"No. I didgeridon't, love," I said. (She didn't get it.) "But I'm looking for a real girl named Oz. About your height. And build. Actually from Australia. Have you seen her?"

And that's pretty much the way it went for days. A barrage of twenties, overpriced drinks, and considerable chafing. I will never understand the appeal of strip clubs, and part of me was hating Oz for making me go on this search in the first place. I was at the end of my rope at FlashDancers today after the latest failed exchange with a Welsh stripper named Misty. I was already doubling up on locations. I headed for the exit as quickly as I could without creating any more friction than necessary in my stripper-grinded jeans.

"Brother, hold up a sec," the bouncer called as I passed.

He was studying me in a way I was not accustomed to. I guess you have to go where you don't belong to feel unique.

"What you after, man?" he asked, chewing on a toothpick.

"I'm looking for a girl from Australia. I can't find her in any of the clubs. She calls herself Oz."

"Shit. Who gave her a dumbass stripper name like that?"

"She's not a stripper."

"Not a stripper. Well, that right there might be your problem."

"I don't know where else to look. She was a webcam girl. I thought she might be looking for work."

"Webcam and strippin' not the same thing. Some of these girls have mad acrobatic skills."

"Right. No offense intended," I said. "Seen anyone like that? Ever-changing punk rock hair colors. Chain-smoking. And, y'know, from Australia?"

"Nah, man, sorry, I can't help. But I'll tell you what I tell everyone who can't find what they're looking for. Head over to the Rule 34 Club."

"Rule 34?"

"That's right. Y'know, Rule 34, like they used to say: if it exists, there's porn of it. I work the door on Fridays. They got everything."

DAY 38. THE RULE 34 CLUB

The bouncer's suggestion was officially my best and only lead, so I began to ask around. Apparently, Rule 34 was a high-end porn club, secretly catering to the most esoteric and craven sexual displays. Things that would make even a German search engine blush. And unlike the rest of the sex trade, it wasn't in Times Square. Instead, Rule 34 operated in the financial district, just off Stone Street, looking quite like an up-scale N.Y. steakhouse. That was part of the appeal: you had a legit reason for being there.

I arrived around seven. The restaurant was filled with many well-tailored Japanese businessmen. Younger day traders congregated around the bar, discernible from the college frat boys they used to be only by receding hairlines and finer clothes.

"Do you require a table, sir?" the maitre d' asked.

I didn't know what to say. People were definitely eating, and there was no obvious back room. Was there a password?

". . . Fidelio?" I asked.

He rolled his eyes. "Or perhaps you'd care to dine on the lower level?" he suggested.

"Yes. That. Thank you."

"Wonderful. Our hostess will seat you."

I was led to the center of the restaurant by a sophisticated and decidedly not flirtatious young woman in a little black dress. When we reached a gold-handled staircase, she pulled back the red velvet rope and, in one fluid motion, gestured downward for my descent.

"Thank you for visiting Rule 34. Your imagination awaits you."

I walked the darkened steps alone until I reached the first of what I came to learn were three circular and segmented lower levels. Each segment held a room of about forty spectators and a brightly lit stage at the center kept the rest of the audience in total anonymous darkness. That's all I could discern from the small square window in the theater's back door.

I approached an information desk in the center of the first level, manned by another attractive, yet decidedly sexless woman, also in a little black dress, sitting behind a table covered in fine red silk. She appeared too thin to successfully menstruate.

"Welcome to Rule 34," she said. "Would you like to fill out a request and entrance form?"

I took the clipboard. There was a hundred-dollar

entrance fee just to begin, and then additional fees depending on the feasibility of your request. I stepped to the side to complete my paperwork, where an impeccably dressed man in his late forties was already scribbling away. After a moment, he deposited his fine gold pen into his suit pocket and handed his form in to Coco. (I'm going to assume her name was Coco.) She took some time to review.

"Okay . . . I will need to get back to you with exact specifics," she said without a trace of judgment. "But I can tell you this is going to require somewhere in the neighborhood of an additional thousand dollars and several days prep time."

He wasn't pleased. You could tell that by the way his color began to match the red of the tablecloth and also because he said, "I am not pleased." That was a bit of a giveaway. Even to me, who had so much Scotch pumping that I was triple-checking my form for errors in case our sexlessly seductive friend were to take issue with my spelling.

"Isn't this supposed to be the Rule 34 Club?" he demanded.

"Yes, sir, but . . ."

"My imagination awaits me?"

"Yes, sir, but fictional characters always require an additional contribution."

"Surely, that can't be unexpected. This is bullshit."

"Sir, if you wanted to watch Lara Croft in a three-way with Batman and Caprica Six from *Battlestar Galactica*, we could easily accommodate you. In fact, that's going on right now in room seventeen. But certain requests take time."

The man checked his watch and exhaled harder than necessary. "Think you can get it done by Friday?"

"Probably, and we have your contact information."

"Fine."

He left a deposit to place his order. As she shuffled her papers, I could just barely discern the description of his request: Cthulhu furiously masturbating.

Yeah, that would do it.

I handed Coco my papers and saw an instant look of relief on her face. I'd simply written "twenty-something Australian punk rock girl."

"Ah, this will be no problem," she said. "And you're in luck. There's actually a show starting in about thirty minutes. Twenty dollars, please."

I sat in the dark of the deceptively elegant and functional theater. The seats were leather, which I imagined cleaned a lot better than cloth. It was almost too dark to find your way without falling, but I guess they weren't sweating too many trip-and-fall lawsuits. After all, who would want to admit where they were at the time of the incident?

The stage was lit and empty, but there were still things to look at. Much like YouTube gave you other suggested videos, or porn sites offered silent GIFs along the margins, each wall of my theater had three plasma screen TVs stacked in a row, mutely revealing what was going on in the other rooms. Barely discernible bodies and images moving in silence. It was hard to be sure, but so help me, I swear that in one of them I saw Screech from *Saved by the Bell* getting dominated by the *Small Wonder* chick.

Right on time, the lights on stage began to swell and bleed while music seeped in. If I'm not mistaken it was a sexier sax-based version of Men at Work's "Down Under". And just as it got to the "six foot four and full of muscles" part, a thought occurred to me: what if it were Oz? Surely, I couldn't watch her. She might have let strangers gawk at her showering online, but this was real life. And I knew her. I couldn't violate her like that. I decided that if those flaring spotlights oozing back and forth from red to blue shone upon Oz when the curtain rose, I would stand on my chair and call out to her. I would take her from here.

But when the show started, I quickly discerned it wasn't Oz. Just some tattoo'd skank getting double-teamed by two guys with Mohawks. The show lasted about twenty minutes, and I stayed until the end. Even when the guys started urinating on her. I hadn't put that on my request form, but it seemed to do good things for the guy two rows ahead of me, and that's when I realized Rule 34 probably had to double up on requests out of necessity.

When it was over, I checked out one of the other rooms I saw in the preview panels. And then another. And that's how it went. Room to room, drink to drink until my flask was empty. And then as a testament to

34's special appeal, I still didn't leave. It was the most successful re-creation of the Internet I'd seen yet. Like looking at one horrible car accident after another, all of which somehow gave you an inexplicable and shameful erection. At around 3:00 A.M., I finally went home vowing never to return to Rule 34, where I had spent hours and hours staring so intently at things I never wanted to see.

DAY 49. OLD-SCHOOL PEEP SHOW

I have spent every day of the last week at Rule 34. If I weren't drinking so heavily I don't think I could live with myself. And frankly, I wasn't built to drink this hard. I can handle functional alcoholism, at best. This full-blown indulgence has my stomach in flames. A fire that can only be doused with more booze that stokes the flame minutes later like those trick birthday candles that are now only bought ironically, or un-ironically by the worst people in the world. Had I been back at the hotel, with just silence and fire, I might have put the bottle down. Or even if I were walking the streets, needing my wits about me to contend with the ever-changing Apocalypse. But I was here. At Rule 34. Distracted from everything outside and above ground. Filling my mind with nothing but head-shakingly awful porn and my body with Scotch. A few days ago, I tried to get my head straight upstairs with a filet mignon. It was expertly prepared, but my body didn't want it, and I had to push it aside after a few bites.

The club was open 24/7, and some days I hadn't even gone home to sleep, catching periodic cat naps in the various theaters after the shows had ended. I hadn't even put in a request since day two. Instead, I just followed the perversity of the suggested viewing, from window to room, window to room. It was cheaper that way anyway. There was only a ten-dollar charge for watching someone else's request. They made the majority of the money catering to special whims like that Cthulhu gentleman. After about a week, I realized I had not spoken to another person in days. Not one word. Just me. Drinking in the dark and lit only by the display before me.

I stumbled from a theater where Smurfette was blowing Gargamel and headed back to the information desk.

"Form please, Coco," I said.

It was a different woman. I think. Same dress and a severe short black haircut. She handed me a clipboard, and I quickly put in my request. She scanned it several times.

"I'm sorry, sir. I don't . . . what is this?"

"What? It's right there. It's what I want."

"But I don't understand—"

"What is this bullshit?" I asked. "You can show us Cthulhu masturbating, Lieutenant Uhura and Agent

Scully getting bi-curious, but I write one simple name and you're giving me shit?"

"I'm not trying to be difficult—"

"It's right there! One name. It's what I want. I'll pay anything!"

"It's not a question of money," she said. "It's—"

"It's what?"

She waited for a moment, and then asked as simply as she could, "Who's Romaya?"

I walked out of 34, needing a shower and two days' sleep. I saw the sun and didn't like it. I thought about the hotel and the no one waiting for me. I kept walking. You couldn't call it lost because I had no destination. And maybe it was luck or maybe it was just my body trying to reboot after having frozen on so many undesirable screens, but I found myself back at the beginning. Right at that shitty costume store/porn shop on Forty-third and Eighth.

But this time, I noticed something different. In addition to the porn, there was a peep show. Old-school girls behind glass. I bought a rubber mask that only covered the nose and eyes so I could still drink, and headed in. The room was small and dark, and reeked of what I hoped was bleach. I took a seat in front of the window, and a young woman with brown hair and glasses sat in a kimono on the other side. She was too pretty to be here.

"What do you want?" she asked.

"I'm not sure."

"Well, what do you like?" She reached over to the small table by her side to crush out a cigarette. "Wanna tell me what you like?"

"I'd prefer not to," I heard myself say.

"Well, my name's Maya," she said, and uncrossed her legs. Her kimono opened slightly, still holding to her breast, but revealing a dolphin tattoo below her waist.

"Hello, Maya," I said. "Will you just sit here with me for a minute?"

"It's your money," she said, and let the kimono open further. "So what should I call you?"

"Call me . . . Gladstone," I said, and took off my mask.

Maya jumped off her chair and closed her kimono.

"What the fuck, Gladstone?!"

I didn't understand. She banged up against the glass, crying. No. Not crying. Happy.

"It's me! Oz!"

7.

DAY 49. RETURN TO OZ

It didn't seem possible that in a world devoid of Facebook, Twitter, and people-finding apps like Foursquare, I had somehow managed to locate a five-foot-five Australian girl among the 700,000 people still living in the city. Even stranger, I hadn't recognized her.

Oz ran from her tiny glass room, clear heels clacking in the hallway, and when she burst through my door, kissing me and holding me tight, I couldn't help but think of Romaya and how we loved each other when we were that young.

"Christ, Gladstone," she said, pulling back suddenly. "Why do you reek of Drakkar Noir?"

Her hair was longer now and flowed in California redwood colors without the distraction of store-bought fluorescents. Sexy librarian glasses had taken the place of disposable contacts. And her accent had somewhat dissolved into a softer dialect of unknown origin. Oz saw the confusion on my face.

"What is it?" she asked. "Have you found Tobey? The Internet?"

I just stared, unsure of what I was trying to remember.

"Maybe we should just get you back to the hotel. You don't look right, and you smell like a New Jersey mall."

Oz filled my head with whispered stories while I slept. Stories about the government releasing her after a brief interrogation, about losing her purse and keys in the arrest, and about how she did visit the hotel in the first three days, but no one answered the door or took her calls. She still couldn't find her friend, and she moved on, looking for work and shelter. I was too tired to respond to any of it. Or maybe it was just a feeling of contentment I didn't want to disturb with words.

In the morning, I woke with Oz straddling my back. "Wake up, old man," she said. "Time to find the Internet."

I rolled over beneath her and placed a hand on each of her thighs. "First we have to get Tobey. It would be too sad to find it without him."

"There's something I want to do even before that,"

she said and leaned over to put her glasses on the nightstand. The soft of her t-shirt caught my stubble.

"What's that? Discuss your daddy issues?"

"I don't have daddy issues."

I slid my hands further up Oz's thighs until she could no longer pretend to be cool.

"In my experience," I said, "women either have daddy issues or a cock."

"Bastard."

She closed her eyes so I couldn't see her smile was everywhere.

Romaya was upset, and I worried about the effect of the stress on our two-week-old baby growing inside her.

"What the fuck?" she said. "This isn't the nineteen-fifties. You don't have to drop out of law school just because I'm pregnant."

"Don't I?" I said. "Fuck this. I need to earn money."

"You will, dumbass. When you're a lawyer."

"That's not for two more years. What 'til then? We gonna move in with your mom in California?"

"We'll do whatever we have to do. We'll do what people do. But you don't have to give up being a law-yer."

"Well, what if I don't want to be a lawyer? What the fuck is a lawyer? Even now, Professor Hollister said she could get me a job at the Workers' Compensation

Board. Isn't that all I want? A job? To be a real live grown-up?"

"I don't know? What do you want?"

"I want to be your husband. I want to be a daddy. And I don't care about any of the rest."

Oz took off her shirt and leaned all the way back with me still inside her. Her hair grazed my ankles, and I licked my thumb before placing it for maximum impact. I stroked the geometry of sex with a confidence unknown in my twenties, and she couldn't stop the words from flowing.

"Fuck me, Daddy," she moaned.

I waited for the taboo of her exclamation to start a chain reaction of reproach. But it didn't. I sat up, swelling inside her and then bared down with my full weight, both my hands on her wrists, holding her down.

"Say that again." My voice rough and warm in her ear.

"Fuck me."

I took my right hand off her wrist just long enough to slap her face. Her gasp interrupting moans.

"Good girl," I said, and laid my body against hers. My hands beneath her shoulders. Fingers curling up and over, pulling her into me.

I was a grown-up. A full-blown man. Even if my baby died inside my wife while she was still my fiancée. Even if that wife was gone now too. Even if the words in this journal will wither, never seeing the light of the Internet. I was in Oz, getting the job done. I was a man.

DAY 50. CRAIGSLIST

Oz smoked her cigarettes, and I smoked her cigarettes too, but after a shower, we set out in search of Tobey. Oz led the way. In our two weeks apart, she had learned all about the latest non-technological advances in our Internet-less world. Much like pornography, knowledge had become too easily obtained and we couldn't go without. We needed our answers to flow more freely than our desire to look for them, and although the Net was gone, other things rose to take its place.

Oz told me that the Library of Congress had hired hundreds of new librarians simply for the purpose of researching and responding to queries. For one dollar, you could fax a question in and, using the resources of America's largest library, the answer would be tracked down and faxed back to you within twenty-four hours. Some of the requested information was more important than others.

"Check your pocket," Oz said.

"What?"

"I got you a present. Gave it to you while you were sleeping."

I reached inside my jacket, keeping my eyes on Oz.

"Go ahead," she reassured me. "It's okay."

I slowly pulled out a piece of paper, folded into fours. It was a fax from the Library of Congress, reading, "From 1982 to 1984 Jason Bateman portrayed Derek Taylor on *Silver Spoons*."

"Aww, thanks," I said.

"Yeah, well, I got tired of hearing you and Tobey bitch about it," she said. "But that shit's nothing compared to Jeeves."

Turns out that if you were fortunate enough to live in New York City—still the greatest city in the world, even if people were leaving in droves and the threat of terrorist attacks increased daily—you had an even more impressive alternative for acquiring information. You could ask Jeeves.

His real name was Dan McCall, but apparently this fifty-year-old former Columbia University librarian now only answered to "Jeeves." He quit his job the week after the Net went down, and every day from noon to four he would roll his tiny stack table, folding chair, and trunk containing reference materials to the Bethesda Fountain in Central Park to answer questions. But Jeeves's greatest resource was his photographic memory filled with limitless details of historical and trivial import. Also, he was psychic. That was apparently a big part of the appeal too.

He charged five dollars a question. If Jeeves could answer you, he kept the money. If he could provide only related information, he gave you back two dollars. And if your query returned no results, your money was refunded. Supposedly, that had never happened unless you asked about the Internet.

"Wow, that's pretty amazing," I said. "How'd you hear about this?"

"Christ, Gladstone. Everyone's heard about it. Have you been doing anything for the last two weeks besides jerking off?"

I took a nip from my flask. "Does drinking count?"

"Fucking lush. Come on, I wanna get to Craigslist before it gets too crowded."

"Craigslist? What happened to Jeeves?"

Oz looked at me with disgust. "Jeeves is where histrionic, thirty-year-old Sheilas go to find out if their boyfriends are ever gonna propose."

I followed Oz to the 4-5-6 subway stop by Union Square. What used to be a promenade for slackers and artists to smoke, sketch, and skateboard had been transformed. Now it was a promenade for slackers to smoke, sketch, skateboard, and tack index cards to a huge cheap plywood wall. Much like the real Craigslist, the board had been separated into sections: jobs, items for sale, sexual seekers. The overall numbers were smaller, but the odds of ending up a leather gimp in someone's basement were about the same.

"This is how I found a roommate when I couldn't get back into the hotel," Oz said.

"Yeah, but how will this help us find Tobey? What kind of post are we looking for? Single White Male seeks eighties references and tits?"

"I dunno, but it couldn't hurt to start looking."

I searched the cards for close to an hour without any leads. Someone had posted a card reading "highly intelligent twenty-something seeks at-home job requiring no work. Hours must be flexible," but that could have been anyone. For the most part, the wall was flooded with ads for antiquated gaming systems. The loss of online gaming and even Flash distractions had left people jonesing for some seated, hand/eye-coordinated entertainment. Somehow, playing Xbox alone and offline was too depressing. Antiques, however, were exciting and novel. Less of a reminder of what was lost. There was a Vectrex from '84 on sale for nine hundred dollars, and even a bunch of games relying on ball, hole, and spring technology were selling for more than I'd ever imagined.

Just before my frustration reached its peak, I felt Oz slip her arms around me from behind and rest her head against my shoulder like my own guardian angel of affection.

"Aww, you still want to ask Jeeves, don't you?" she said.

Ask Jeeves

Oz and I took a long slow walk to Central Park, pretending a life was possible supported only by my disability payments and her rack-based ability to earn extra cash on an as-needed basis. It was the kind of fragile new infatuation that let simple answers carry more weight than they deserved because further exploration would send the whole thing tumbling down.

"Do you think you'll ever go back to work?" she would ask.

"I prefer not to," I'd reply. "What's your real name?"

"Isn't it sexier not knowing?"

"Who's your friend in New York?"

It was 2:00 P.M. by the time we reached the park, and the line to Jeeves was already fifty people deep. A bunch of Internet zombies were milling about in their circles, but most of them gave Jeeves a wide berth for fear of accidentally obtaining some actual knowledge. He sat there with his balding ponytail and poorly defined goatee, dispensing information from a folding chair. Sometimes he consulted his books—the *OED* or an encyclopedia. Sometimes he grabbed the person's hand to answer the more personal, psychic-based questions. But usually he would just roll his eyes in disgust and dispense answers one by one while collecting his money.

Q: "What's the average yearly rainfall in the
      Amazon rain forest?"
A: "Six feet, seven inches."
Q: "Will I ever find a job I don't hate?"
A: "No."
Q: "Is there a God?"

A: "I don't know if a God exists, but anyone who claims to be certain of His absence probably lacks humility more than faith."

Jeeves gave the God guy back two of his five dollars on that one and whistled "Onward Christian Soldiers" as he placed the remaining three in his lockbox.

A skinny sixteen-year-old boy came up next, dropping five singles on the table.

"Where's the Internet?" he asked.

Jeeves's arrogance gave way to irritation. "I get that question every single day. I don't know."

"But you know everything. How can you not know?"

"Well, I don't, okay?" he said, pulling down on the rising edges of his *Dark Side of the Moon* t-shirt.

The boy reached to take back his five dollars, and Jeeves stopped him.

"Only take two," he said.

"Why?" the boy asked. "You haven't told me anything."

"I don't know where the Internet is, but I just felt something. . . . There is someone who will find it."

Jeeves stood and held up his hands as if absorbing psychic visions through his palms.

"I can feel it. I can see him. In my mind. There will be . . . for lack of a better phrase . . . an Internet Messiah. He will come. And he will return the Net to us."

Jeeves sat down, spent from his pronouncement. A buzz worked its way through the crowd. A couple of

YouTube zombies were even distracted enough to let their trapped cat run off to freedom. For a moment, it seemed all of Central Park was quiet.

"You're not just saying that so you can keep three of my dollars, are you?"

"Next!" Jeeves screamed, and within a moment, he was back to spewing answers. "Hammerin' Hank Greenberg; The Articles of Confederation; leave it alone or it will get infected; no, he will never marry you; Jason Bateman . . ."

We continued advancing as Jeeves dispatched about thirty people, until only a few stood between us. From our new place in line we could now only hear the questions.

"Okay, Jeeves," someone said. "Question. Who would give better head: 1977 Lynda Carter or 2001 Angelina Jolie?"

"Are they dressed as Wonder Woman and Lara Croft, respectively?"

"Of course!"

"Well," Jeeves said. "It's a cliché, but I have to go with Angelina Jolie."

"Wrong! The answer is Demi Moore as G.I. Jane, but keep the money, Mr. Know-It-All."

I didn't need the crowd to clear to know I'd found Tobey. And not just because of his Demi Moore infatuation, but because this was someone who managed to take pride in stumping an educated psychic with a completely subjective and arbitrary question. Still, I can't tell you how happy I was to see the goofy bastard. I rushed to the front, and we screamed and hugged and punched each other the way you do when your emotions are greater than your arsenal of clichés.

"Fuck, am I happy to see you," he said. "I just spent my last five dollars."

"You spent your last five dollars to ask Jeeves a blowjob question?"

"I know," Tobey said. "Now I can't get that Jaguar."

"Seriously, Tobes. How did you manage to survive New York for two weeks without me?"

It seems Tobey had gotten a job tending bar at Stand Up NY and spent the rest of his time barking tickets in the street in exchange for a place to stay. Apparently, the manager had been a big fan of his blog.

The loss of the Web had changed the stand-up scene. More and more comics were going retro with Henny Youngman-style one liners. At first, Tobey thought that the loss of the Net had people nostalgic for a simpler time. But after a few days, he realized the comics were merely using all the Tweets they couldn't spew to their followers. Seeming to take special delight from the phenomenon, Tobey told me about one night when Rob Delaney and Michael Ian Black did a combined two hours with every joke weighing in at fewer than 140 characters.

"Really?" I asked. "How was that?"

"Retarded. How do you think it was?"

"Well . . ."

"Actually," Tobey said, "I did hear one good one:

'FYI to ladies trying to distinguish yourselves by playing hard to get: sucking cock better also works.'"

I laughed. "Who wrote that one?"

"I did," Tobey said. "Right now. Fuck, I miss Twitter."

I was about to respond, but I suddenly felt consumed by an overwhelmingly antsy and negative energy. I turned to the woman behind me, who was about thirty years old and filled with venom.

"Are you going to go?" she asked. "Some of us have important questions about our boyfriends."

"Save your money," Oz said. "With an attitude like that I'm sure you turned him gay long ago."

The line ahead of us had cleared, and Jeeves was tapping his fleshy fingers, waiting for me.

"Oh, I'm sorry," I said. "My question got answered already."

Jeeves stood up and pointed, but his words did not come.

"Look, no offense. I was just searching for this jackass here, and I found him, so . . ."

"It's you!" Jeeves stammered.

"I'm not sure—"

"You're here."

The crowd that already hung on Jeeves's every word was now listening more closely than ever. They began to circle the table.

"It's him!" he screamed. "It's the Internet Messiah!"

8.

DAY 50. THE INTERNET MESSIAH

Sometimes you just do things without knowing why.
When Jeeves dubbed me the Internet Messiah, I
started running. Maybe it was because he had seemed
so collected and self-possessed moments before and
now was gasping for words and pointing at me in
spasmodic fits. Maybe it was the hunger clawing out
from the sunken eyes of the YouTube zombies. Or
maybe it was the crippling attention of Central Park.
But I ran as fast and as far as I could, and Tobey and
Oz, either possessed by the same spirit or just trying
to look after me, followed.

It wasn't hard to outrun Jeeves. He started cough-
ing and spitting after only a few steps, but from the
bouncing blur of my peripheral vision, I could see in-

quisitive pedestrians take his place. They turned and pointed and joined the herd one by one. Oz kept pace with me, dressed more functionally today in a pair of jeans and Doc Martens. Tobey was hauling ass a few steps behind with a huge grin on his face.

"You think this is *A Hard Day's Night* or something?" I called over my shoulder.

"I don't know what that is."

"I hate you, Tobey."

We ran past the joggers and baby strollers. The Hacky Sackers and caricaturists. The lovers taking walks and married couples washing off dropped pacifiers with bottled water. But by the time we got to the dude selling Tweety Bird ice-cream pops out of his pushcart, the YouTube zombies had started closing in. Tobey reached down for a fallen branch without breaking stride and swung it around across a zombie's face. Everything froze before the crack had even stopped reverberating through the park. Oz and I watched to see what would happen next, as did the chasers slowly circling.

The zombie, on all fours and bleeding from the mouth, made a horrible groan as he reached up and out. Tobey brought the remnants of the branch over his head and was about to swing again when I screamed out, "What are you doing?"

"What?" Tobey replied. "I gotta destroy the brain!"

"You realize that's not a real zombie, right? It's just an expression."

"C'mon! Is this the Internet Apocalypse or what?" Tobey asked.

"He's not the undead," Oz explained. "It's just an Internet-addicted human who—"

Unfortunately, she had to cut her explanation short because in the time it took to down one zombie, twenty more had crept in and their circle was almost completely around us.

"Run," I said. "And don't fucking stop."

I sprinted as hard as I could through the one opening in the enclosing group and headed north. I could hear Oz and Tobey on my heels, but I didn't look to check. After about five minutes at full speed, Tobey called out for a break, but I kept running. The Swedish Cottage was coming into view. I remembered the cottage from walks with Romaya. It was over 130 years old and, according to its sign out front, had served as a WWII civil defense headquarters, a tool house, a library, and now, a marionette theater. It was at the upper end of the park, and for some reason that meant something. Maybe because breaking out from the trees seemed like freedom. I'd never seen zombies in taxis or subways.

Oz called out to me with the desperation Tobey lacked, and I had to look. She was holding Tobey up, and he was dripping with sweat, ready to hurl. Apparently, his running habits were like his blogging: best for impressive sprints and incompatible with marathons. He held on to Oz, hunched over and sucking wind while limping toward me. I scanned our surroundings. We seemed to have outrun the zombies. What they had in a focused determination, they lacked in proper nutrition. Although, it seemed my steady diet of Scotch hadn't slowed me down.

I helped Oz, keeping Tobey between us with his arms around both our shoulders, his right hand gripping me for support, his left hand hanging limp and, arguably, caressing Oz's left breast more than absolutely necessary.

"Let's just sit down for a sec," he said, pointing to a bench outside the cottage.

"We can't stop until we're out of this park."

"He's right, Tobes," Oz said. "And how the fuck is a skinny guy like you so out of shape anyway?"

"Sssh," Tobey said. "Or I'll start to doubt the cardio benefits of constantly being high."

Then he threw up across the entrance of the cottage, and sat down on the bench anyway.

"Cri—Christ!" Oz exclaimed, jumping a foot from the spew.

"You were gonna say 'crikey,' weren't you?" I asked.

Oz denied it with a defiant three syllable "No-o-o."

"You were totally gonna say crikey," Tobey agreed, spitting out the remains of what I imagined was lunch. "And may I also offer, I don't think we should head north anymore. Or south."

I turned around to see nearly fifty Internet zombies closing in from all directions. I pulled on the main door to the cottage, but it was locked.

"Quick. Give me a bobby pin," I said to Oz.

"It's 2014. Who the fuck has a bobby pin? You think I keep it with my emery boards and curlers?"

They were getting closer. I took the pen from the pages of my journal and popped the clip off to make a tension wrench.

"I need something like a bobby pin. A paper clip. Anything."

Oz started feeling around in her backpack and scavenging the ground.

"Will a paper clip work?" Tobey asked, pulling that and some change from his pocket.

I had no time to hate him. And not just because zombies were approaching from thirty feet, but because of the jolt of déjà vu as I took the clip. Suddenly, I was with Romaya and Martin in my law school dorm, working another window. The one on the twentieth floor in the hallway that led to the roof. I stood on top of a radiator to pick the window's top lock as Martin worked the bottom. Romaya kept watch, just like Oz was doing now, except she was looking for RAs coming around the corner instead of approaching Internet zombies. Martin popped his lock first and passed his superior paper clip pick up to me.

A moment later, I popped mine, too, and we had access to the roof. I took a step out of the dorm and into the air, completely aware that I had lived my very short life in such a rule-based way that this simple act of rebellion was clearly the worst thing I'd ever done. The night welcomed me, wet and black like a Morphine song, and I offered Romaya my hand as she slipped out as happy as I'd ever seen her, somehow collecting all the darkness in the flow of her hair.

"Look! The stories," she said, pointing to the apartment building across the way.

Martin didn't understand, but I knew Romaya was just trying to get closer. Closer to those storybook lives we'd watched from my window. And now, on the edge, there was nothing between us besides New York City air and time. They were closer then ever.

"For fuck's sake, Gladstone," Oz screamed. "They're closer than ever."

I dragged my pick across the lock's teeth, hoping they would catch. A ripple of metal and then nothing. I did it again. Harder, but slower, while focusing on my former law school grace until I heard a click.

"Get in here," I screamed, opening the door.

Oz and Tobey ran into the Swedish Cottage, and I locked the door behind us. I'd done it. We were inside. There was a stage and some benches. There were also lots of windows. Zombie hands slapped at the panes while hungry fingers scratched at the doors.

"Secure the entrances!"

"With what?" Tobey asked.

"I don't know. Plywood!" I barked.

"Um, yeah. I'm pretty sure most puppet theaters don't keep stacks of plywood and nails in case of zombie attack," Tobey said.

"Well, this place used to be a toolshed. Surely, there's something?"

"Surely?" Oz asked. "You don't think they managed

to relocate the axes and *Evil Dead* chain saws when they converted this to a puppet theater?"

"Fuck off," I said. "I picked the lock. You do something."

That's when a rock came through the window. Then another. Then some more. In fact, the rocks kept coming even after every piece of glass was shattered. That's the thing with zombies. Total herd mentality.

In the few minutes that followed the first broken window, the three of us did our best to arm ourselves, but managed to gather little more than rocks and puppets. And then they were in. About fifty, all approaching.

"Will you bring us Facebook?" a sixteen-year-old girl asked.

"Twitter first!" her friend demanded. "I have no idea what Justin Bieber's been doing."

"No, I'm sorry, but no. I can't do any of that," I said, backing up to the stage.

"When can I stream Netflix again?"

"Can you bring back *World of Warcraft* right where I left off? I was just about to hit the level cap!"

"Please, I'd love to have the Internet too, and I'm looking for it, but I don't know any more than you."

"Why are you even here?" one teenage boy asked. "Shouldn't you be getting the Internet? It's been weeks, and you're the Messiah."

"I've just explained—"

My attempt to make myself understood was interrupted by a fat man in sweatpants. "Please!" he screamed, grabbing my lapels and driving me against the hard wood of the stage. Then he fell to his knees and whispered, ". . . I can't afford the Rule 34 Club."

"I can't help you. I'm sorry. I'm not this Internet Messiah. I'm just some guy."

"He's lying!" a Digg zombie called out. "He wants it for himself. It's a conspiracy!"

"Yeah, himself and Corporate America!" a Reddit zombie agreed.

"Give it to us!"

The group closed in as if I could produce the Internet from my inside coat pocket if they just pressed hard enough. This would end badly. Especially since no matter how hard they beat me, I would never be able to give them what they needed. I simply didn't have it to give, and more than the fear of being torn apart by a crowd, I couldn't bear to see the disappointment in their eyes. Another promise broken. I had to find a way out.

I climbed up on the stage, raising a unicorn puppet I'd grabbed, above my head. "Wait! All of you. You don't need to walk around endlessly waiting for the world to come online. We can entertain ourselves."

"How?" Twitter girl asked.

"I don't know. Plays, theater, music?"

"Are you seriously gonna put on some sort of gay puppet show?"

Seeing my desperation, Tobey got up on the stage with a lion puppet.

"Look at me," he exclaimed. "I'm Farty McPooPoo, the gassy lion!"

That played well with the kids, but some of the crowd frowned, seeming to exhibit more discriminating taste. Oz got on stage with a princess puppet.

"And I'm Princess Scat-lover! Mmmm, come here, Farty McPoo-Poo."

Farts and deviant sex. Now we were on to something. The crowd closed in, gathering tight around the stage. There was no way out, and I couldn't imagine the adventures of the Dirty Princess and Her Farty Lion would last forever.

"Z'oh, my God," Tobey cried, and pointed off in the distance. "Look!"

I couldn't believe Tobey was trying to fool an angry mob with the oldest trick in the book. It was probably because he didn't really read books. But then I saw fifty faces turn, and what's more, it wasn't a trick at all. As if proof of some higher power, there, in the middle of Central Park, was a kitten dressed as a Daft Punk robot trained to dance to "Get Lucky" while its owner, a shapely burlesque dancer in a leopard-print bikini, Bettie Page wig, and heels danced along behind. It was the ultimate living Internet meme and the masses drew to it like moths to a flame or Web reporters to secret gay sex.

Oz and I stared in disbelief as the crowd thinned, leaving us alone. Then we noticed Tobey leaving too.

"Tobey!" I hissed.

"Dude," he said. "Do you not see this shit? Look at it."

"Yeah, it's great. Do you mind if we run away now? Because getting consumed by zombies sounds like a drag."

Oz and I slowly edged toward the door and Tobey reluctantly followed. Just as we broke into a run, I could have sworn I saw Agent Rowsdower peek from behind a tree, but I wasn't turning to make sure. I needed to get away to some place where no one needed anything from me.

We broke free of the park and hopped a subway to some miserable Upper West Side bar I knew from my Fordham law orientation bar crawl. Tobey was looking decidedly less green after some beers and nachos, and with nearly no cannabis in his system for twelve hours, he was finding purpose.

"So," he said, picking the best nacho to systematically snag every other cheese-connected chip, "where to, Mr. Messiah?"

I guess it was a normal question, but it caught me by surprise.

"We just escaped a park full of zombies," I said. "I thought we might, y'know, chill for a bit."

"Yeah, that was pretty crazy. You have more followers now than you ever did on Twitter."

"Yeah, I never really got Twitter," I confessed.

"Well, reading Twitter's a lot like staring at an ant

farm," Tobey explained while wiping some cheese from his mouth. "Except without all the productivity."

"And the ants hate themselves," Oz added.

"So anyway," Tobey continued when the laugh died down. "Get your drink on and all that, but then, after that. Where's next on our journey?"

Oz touched me under the table.

"I'm not sure, Tobes," I said, biting the Scotch out of my ice. "So . . . what about tonight? You sleeping at Stand Up NY?"

"Well, I was, but . . ."

Tobey's eyes scanned back and forth between Oz and me. "Holy fuck," he yelled. "You fuckers are fucking, aren't you?"

Bits of spewed chips littered the table.

"Aren't you?" he insisted.

"Sorry, Tobes," I said. "There were a lot of fucks in there, I'm still working out the syntax."

"What if we are?" Oz said.

"But Gladstone's old enough to be your dad!"

"I really wasn't getting any at thirteen, Tobey."

"That's not the point. Bros before hos, G-Stone!" Then Tobey turned meekly to Oz. "No offense."

"Don't be silly," Oz said, spearing the lime in her vodka tonic. "Why would I be offended?"

"I just mean . . ." Tobey took a second to swallow his food. "We're on a journey here."

"No one's forgetting the journey, Tobes. It's just, I don't know, maybe it's time to regroup. If we split up for a few days and then pool resources . . ."

"Oh, fuck off. Just hang a tie on the door and spare me this bullshit."

He got up from the table.

"Tobey, it's not like that—"

"Well, I'm still looking," he said. "I'll be sure to report back with my findings."

And then he was gone.

"He'll be back," Oz said. "And at least this time we know where to find him."

"Just don't talk for a second, Yoko."

"Excuse me," Oz said. "What incredibly dated reference are you making?"

"Y'know, The Beatles broke up before I was born, too, right?"

"Yeah, I know," Oz said. "My musical knowledge doesn't start with Midnight Oil."

In the early days, Romaya used to wake around 7:00 A.M. and whisper, "Hello, in there," directly into my ear, over and over, until she had a playmate. Oz seemed more the sleep-in type, and she didn't start to stir until I did. My half-dreamed attempts at snuggle sex succeeded only in turning on the TV. One of us must have rolled on the remote.

It was that Fox News morning news show with the Stepford wife, the lanky homophobic gay guy, and the third dude of unknown, swarthier origin playing clips from Bill O'Reilly's broadcast the night before.

"Isn't that a picture of Jeeves?" Oz asked, pointing.

It was. Apparently, O'Reilly had interviewed Jeeves about his Internet Messiah prophesies. I sat up, hoping not to be national news.

Jeeves had cleaned up only slightly. A short-sleeved button-down shirt, khakis with frayed hems, and Birkenstocks. Not the best look, but I'd never seen a man with less to prove, so I'm sure it didn't matter.

"My vision is very clear, Mr. O'Reilly. And this is not something I'm trying to profit from, but, yes, to answer your question, for the lack of a better word, I do believe there is an 'Internet Messiah' and he will return the Net to us."

"How?"

"I'm not sure."

"Who is he?"

"I'm not sure."

"But you're sure this Internet Messiah exists?"

"Yes, I have seen him."

O'Reilly didn't try to hide his disdain. "You're a Columbia University librarian, aren't you?"

"I was."

"Oh, that's right. Was. You went into this Ask Jeeves business when the Net died."

"I did."

"Your real name's Dan McCall."

"That is also true, but these days I prefer Jeeves."

O'Reilly had had enough. "Um, Mr. Jeeves, if I have to call you that, why should I believe any of this?"

Jeeves sat forward in his chair. "Well, Bill, I guess

it doesn't really matter if you believe me or not, but for everybody else—who won't be dead within three days—I am telling the truth."

Fox then cut back to the morning anchors.

"What did that mean?!" the hostess asked.

"Please," said the tall guy. "Did you see the state of his khakis? New York apparently has no shortage of crazy."

"Well, you caught a break there, old man," Oz said, nuzzling into my chest. "No one's taking Jeeves seriously."

Not that there was much to take seriously, but Oz was right. These were desperate days, and it wouldn't be the first time people believed a thirty-something Jew could lead them to salvation.

"Where do you feel like going today, lady?" I asked.

"I'm not leaving this bed."

"Okay," I said. "But tomorrow, we look for the Net. I told Tobey we would, and I wasn't lying. I don't want to lie to Tobey."

"Tomorrow."

DAY 53. THE MUSEUM

I've been lying to Tobey. For the second time in a month, I've spent days in this hotel. Not out of fear or withdrawal, but just because I could. The booze was flowing, Oz was sensational, and best of all, I slept. I slept the way I hadn't slept since Romaya—where you're completely dead to the world, but not oblivious. You can't be oblivious. It's the knowing that someone is right next to you that lets you fall so far away.

But when I woke, I knew I'd hate myself if I spent one more day doing nothing.

"Pack your Vegemite," I said. "We're going to the Museum of Natural History."

"You think stuffed animals stole the Internet?" Oz replied.

"First off, they're not stuffed, they're real animal skins pulled taut over carved wood, and second, I'll let you in on a little secret: I'm not the Internet Messiah. I have no idea where the Internet is, but I'm pretty sure it's not in your vag."

I've always loved the Museum of Natural History. With the exception of the giant whale room, it hasn't changed since I was a kid. Or even for fifty years before that. And it doesn't need to. Neither television nor Atari nor *World of Warcraft* has tarnished its ability to captivate. And I don't really know why. Something about the architecture, the lighting, and the layout transforms these animal-quins behind century-old glass into something otherworldly. Magic is a cliché, but what do you call it when you enter a place and you can pretend you're anywhere and everywhere from the Mesozoic era to present day, provided you haven't killed every bit of childhood wonder with cynicism? It is magic. The kind that exists.

Or maybe it's knowing you're seeing what your grandfather saw, the way he saw it. The same stimuli are firing your synapses in the same way they worked some little boy's brain in 1912. It's a rock of consistency in the fastest-changing city in the world. But the best part is that you can spend all day there without learning a damn thing. Staring at the dinosaurs and statues, feeling the flow of the space, and ignoring the explanatory cards and postings. It's like surfing the Net at 2:00 A.M. without the capacity for thought. But the difference is, by the time you leave the museum, you know that knowledge exists and that it deserves to be showcased and exalted. So the real magic is that even walking the museum passively informs your priorities—a philosophical education if not a factual one.

I showed Oz the giant spider crab that terrorized my childhood dreams. We lingered over the Peter Stuyvesant mannequin my mother had shown me on a parent-chaperoned school field trip, just as it had been shown to her when she was a schoolgirl. The history was kind of lost on Oz.

"Oh, I guess in your country, it would be a lot more mannequins getting prison raped, huh?"

"Seriously," she said. "Do you know anything about Australia?"

"Of course not. Facts would only ruin my jokes."

We spent nearly the whole day there. Oz was taken by the section with the dinosaur bones, which, for reasons that have never been clear to me, also contained a bear skeleton. She started laughing when we reached that part.

"What?"

"It reminds me of you."

"Y'know, I can't help it that I don't have any shins. You think I like putting my shoes on my kneecaps?"

"Aww, bears are cute."

We continued on to the evolution section, and I couldn't pretend I was on anything other than a date, but I also felt this was more than a pleasure trip. That I could honestly report to Tobey that I'd learned something on this part of the journey. Something for the journal, even if I still had no idea what that was.

"I'm getting hungry," Oz said. "I could eat the arse out of a dead 'roo."

"Did you really just say that?"

"What? It's an expression."

"Christ, you people are ridiculous."

"Ridiculous and hungry."

We made our way to the exit, ending a beautiful day, but still waiting to learn whatever it was that I felt was coming. I hoped Tobey was just fucking off and getting high, because I was feeling increasingly guilty about taking three days off from our mission, but I felt he wasn't. That diner exchange was the closest I'd ever come to fighting with Tobey. I'd never seen him with that level of determination. Eventually, he'd come find me or I'd find him, and I wanted to have something to report when that happened.

Outside, the street was filled with ambulances and police cars, and I assumed there was yet another terror alert. It was becoming a familiar scene in the city. Soldiers on bullhorns directing pedestrians away from certain public buildings. Closed subway lines. Instant congestion by sudden road closings. For many, city life had become incredibly difficult. But those were mostly people with jobs and places to go. We were just trying to get a burger. And it wasn't terrorist activity we were seeing after all. Just a really bad car accident.

Ordinarily, I wouldn't sit around and gawk, but I did. And Oz did too, despite her arse-munching hunger, because new salacious details kept flowing. We learned the driver was drunk. There was opened booze in the car. And while he'd been killed, his passenger was still alive. She said they were late for an anti-abortion rally. Others said they must have been going over seventy when they crashed into that limo. And that was the other thing. There was a dead limo passenger too. Bill O'Reilly.

9.

DAY 55. IDOLATERS AND THE DEVOUT

O'Reilly's death tore through the television media with all the right/left jabs of grief and dark humor you'd expect. But the surprising part was that even without the clip-circulating power of the Internet, it was only hours before people started reporting that Jeeves's prediction had come true. O'Reilly was dead within three days of the interview. In the next twenty-four hours, Jeeves went from a local celebrity and national wingnut to a legit psychic. *The New York Times* reported: "Local Psychic Predicts O'Reilly Death." The *New York Post* headline was less subtle: "O'Reilly? Oh, Really! Crackpot Jackpot!"

It didn't take long for people to turn to Jeeves's other prophesies. He'd become the man with the path to the messiah of e-salvation. Fortunately, he didn't know who I was, and only fifty or so zombies had seen my face. People were just looking for the Messiah, not necessarily me. Jeeves told the media he still felt my presence in New York, but could give no details. Still, he was taking blind walks through the city with half-closed eyes and arms outstretched, and an increasing number of zombies and people with too much free time had started following him. I wasn't sure how he got lucky on O'Reilly, but whatever psychic powers he was claiming to have were leading his ass all around the Upper West Side, so I wasn't overly concerned.

I was more troubled by my lack of progress. Almost two months into my journey, and I was no closer to finding the Net than when I started. I turned to my list of "suspects." Corporate America, Terrorists, the Government. My investigation was more pathetic than I'd imagined. I'd spent more time jerking off, drinking, and fucking than gathering clues. I sat alone with my journal, which was nearly devoid of information, while Oz showered, and thought about my one lead: the detection of Internet activity somewhere downtown and/or on Staten Island. I needed Tobey. Yes, he sniffed leads without discretion like an overzealous puppy, but that was something. And even rejecting his ideas carried some worth in itself. Got the wheels turning. I needed him.

And then he was there. A knock at my door answering my deepest wishes. I opened it without even checking (which was probably a good idea, since I still hadn't recovered from the time Tobey managed to drop his pants and do a handstand for the sole purpose of giving me a peephole full of his fish-eyed junk).

Tobey looked good. Eyes not all dilated and bloodshot. Clear-headed and focused right when I was so lost. I dragged Tobey into the room with a hug that was as hard as I missed him, because I knew neither of us was stupid enough to say "no homo."

"I'm sorry, Tobey," I said. "I'm glad you're back."

"Yeah, me too, G-Balls."

He started eating from a bag of pretzels on the dresser.

"I don't know what I'm doing, Tobes."

"Fuck, you mean you're not the Internet Messiah?"

"Sorry."

"It's okay, Gladdy. I've been on the job. Guess where I'm working; you'll never guess."

Tobey kept staring and waiting.

"What? You said I'd never guess!"

"You're useless. The United Nations."

"How the hell did you get a job at the UN?"

"Told you you'd never guess. Well, one of us had to be a detective. What about foreign governments? You been investigating those?"

"No, but I would think the UN would have, like, a huge background check."

"Have you listened to anything I've been telling you, Gladstone? We're off the grid. We can be who we want. Don't you know that every single disgraceful thing I've ever done has happened online? I don't rob liquor stores. I make tasteless jokes about how I'd rather skull-fuck Demi Moore's eye socket than let Miley Cyrus blow me. I download pornography weeks away from being criminal. Or just a thumb away from criminal if we're talking amazing penetrations and the purity laws of some of our southern states. But in real life, I'm clean. I mean, look at me."

There he was. Oversized sagging shorts, t-shirt, and baseball hat. Twenty-nine and looking nineteen. An almost-angelic baby face of soft skin smiling out from under shaggy, dirty blond hair.

"This is bigger than some 'clear private data.' We're free from our cookies in a way I still don't think you understand."

"So the background check . . ."

"What could they find? Nothing."

"Yeah, but what did you say you did? What qualifies you to work at the UN?"

"Well, first off, take it easy. I'm just an intern. But I have been writing a blog for the last few years on third world debt forgiveness, rape in Darfur, the rain forest and—"

"And there's no way to call bullshit."

"Right, and it's kinda true. I had some rape in Darfur jokes on my site. But enough of that. We have an Internet to find. So, y'know, grab your crocodile huntress and let's start walking."

Oz emerged a few minutes later, wearing tight

cutoff jeans, Doc Martens, and a t-shirt. They smiled politely at each other and took inventory, making sure there were no hidden dangers in this reunion.

"It's nice to see you, Tobes," she said. "You look well."

"You too. Quick question, though. Did you get a boob reduction?"

"No, but thank you."

"Hmm . . . well something's different," he said. "Why do I want to fuck you less?"

Oz was diplomatic. "Well, you can only suppress your latent homosexuality for so long, Tobes. But I'll tell you what, if you help us find the Internet, I'll be sure to wear something sexually retarded for you really soon."

"Deal!" Tobey exclaimed, and extended his hand to shake on it.

"So, we got everything we need?" Oz asked. "We good to go?"

I checked my flask.

"Maybe we should hit the bottle-o?" Oz suggested.

"The fuck is a 'bottle-o'?" Tobey asked.

"It's a liquor store," I said.

Tobes looked at me.

"Oh fuck. I'm turning Australian."

Despite Oz's suggestion, we walked on without drugs (or much of a destination) and were rewarded for our fearlessness. There was no sign of Jeeves or any would-be disciples of the Internet Messiah. I was still free to walk the streets as unnoticeable as my companions. It was like living online: seen by all and still unknown. And perhaps because we had no destination, we ended up at the center of it all in Midtown. Or maybe that's just where the streets became unwalkable.

Hundreds of people filled Madison Avenue in front of St. Patrick's Cathedral for a demonstration I couldn't identify. A giant red banner containing the letters "CAM" towered over an empty podium on a make-shift stage.

"What does CAM stand for?" I asked.

"No idea," Tobey replied. "Caucasians Against Mexicans?"

"That's retarded."

"What?" Tobey protested. "Do you see how white this rally is?"

I shook my head.

"Well, you guess then."

The crowd burst into applause, and a woman I recognized but could not name took the stage. She wore a smart red business suit and had long, straight black hair. Each of her features was overly defined: her eyes lined in black, her red lips rising to sharp points at the corners, and a game show hostess nose that could easily take out an eyeball during the kinds of passionate sex she clearly never had.

A somewhat rotund but prancy man followed behind her, leading with his hips and waving to the crowd with more wrist action than was absolutely necessary. Context dictated that he was her husband, but appearances would suggest that that should have been impossible. Their three children followed: two girls and a boy, all in blue, and all in a row, smiling, waving, looking happy in a way I never have been. Maybe because my happiness has never been super-imposed over the frozen expression of some witnessed atrocity.

"I was gonna go with Chlamydia-Afflicted Mothers," I said. "But I'm just not feeling it now."

"What is wrong with you?" Oz asked. "We're outside a cathedral. It has to be something like Catholics Against Masturbation."

"Better," I said, "but I can't believe that would get this good a turnout. Besides, I know this chick. She's not Catholic."

Turns out there was a reason she looked familiar. According to the announcement, it was Pennsylvania's junior senator, Melissa Bramson. I'd seen her on news shows, garnering praise from both the Tea Party for her down-homey appeal and the Moral Majority for her Jesus-love/homosexuality-hate combination platter. Her husband, in fact, was a preacher of some kind whose foundation "cured" gays through Bible study. And while I'm sure he preferred to close his eyes and think of Jesus while procreating with his wife, I'm not sure that's technically a cure. Melissa took the podium and her family sat in the seats behind her.

"Welcome," she said. "Welcome to the first rally of Christians Against the Messiah!"

The crowd exploded with applause.

"Wow. I did not see that coming," I said.

"Why would Christians be against the messiah?" Tobey asked.

"The Internet Messiah, jackass," Oz replied.

"Still," I said. "They really didn't think that one through."

Melissa gripped the edges of her podium. "Friends, thank you all so much for coming. I'm so happy to see you all, but I'm here to remind you that these are serious times. Not just because we've lost the Internet, which—gotta tell ya—I'm not so sure that's a bad thing.

"Y'see, that loss just presents a challenge. God has taken away that crutch that we've clung too tightly to and asked us to begin again. To return to a simpler time. You don't need the Internet to play with your kids. You don't need the Internet to take a walk with your spouse. You don't need the Internet to—"

"—pretend your husband isn't jerking off to old Ricky Martin videos," Tobey interrupted.

"You went with Ricky Martin on that one?" I asked.

"Yeah, so?"

"Little too on the nose, I think."

"Yeah, probs."

Melissa continued. "The Internet is not our God. There is only one true Lord and it's not a bunch of wires and buttons. He was here before the Internet and He's here now without it. In this time of darkness, lost jobs, terror threats, I turn to the Holy Father and find my balance. I find my friend. I find—"

"—my husband sodomizing a young man during Bible therapy?" I added.

The tall, middle-aged woman standing in front of us turned around with fiery military precision and glared down. She looked not unlike a well-fed Ann Coulter.

"Y'know, I can hear everything you're saying."

"Wow. Just like Jesus," Oz gasped.

"Yeah, about that, ma'am," Tobey interjected. "Why did Jesus let the Net go offline?"

The woman wasn't sure if she was being mocked, but she wasn't going to miss an opportunity to talk about the majestic mysteries of God's plan.

"Who knows? But when God shuts a door, he opens a window."

"I see," Tobey said. "So God's pretty clearly getting high in his dorm room."

I laughed harder than maybe ever.

"Real nice," she said, as if her words were somehow more insulting, and moved closer to people of finer moral character.

And then the crowd grew quiet. Something had changed in the air. Melissa was taking a dramatic pause, looking up at the heavens as if her old bowling partner lived there, and then gazing out over the settling mob.

"But in these dark times, my friends, there is another distraction. One who would turn our eyes from heaven. A false prophet."

Boos rose forth from the masses. Actual "boos." It was one of the scariest things I'd ever heard.

"You know who I'm talking about. This so-called Internet Messiah. He would have you turn to him during crisis. He professes to lead the way. To bring back the Internet of pornography and gossip. To return the Facebook of adultery. The Myspace of pedophilia . . . "

"The Craigslist of consensual fisting?" Tobey offered.

"And what of this charlatan Jeeves?" Melissa asked. "As surely as he feels the Messiah's presence in New York, I feel this Messiah's bad intentions."

Oz turned to me with feigned indignation. "She feels your bad intentions? And you told me no one ever gave your junk a nickname!"

Now the crowd was getting antsy, distracted by a catalyzed hatred for a man who not only never asked for followers, but who didn't exist. Jeeves had made me a savior. Melissa had made me a devil. I was neither, and it just did not matter. The truth was too ambiguous.

I'd often said that trying to make a point online is like playing a game of telephone with fifty friends. All of whom are deaf. And neurologically impaired. But, in truth, the problem wasn't the Internet; it was people. And even in a crowd of like-minded followers on the receiving end of a simplistic fairy tale, the point was being missed.

"Let's get this Messiah," someone shouted. "He stole the Internet!"

A magnetic rage flowed from that rallying cry, dragging every last scrap of metallic pain and anger from the crowd. They set forth like good Christian soldiers hell-bent on destroying something they had never seen.

10.

DAY 55. PRIVATE INVESTIGATION

When the Christians started storming, we stood to the side and watched them go. Not just because it was fun to see the collected hive mind get grated to pieces by New York's intersecting streets, but because we were scared.

"They fucking hate you," Tobey said when the last zealot disappeared from sight.

"What if they find you?" Oz asked.

"How could they? Jeeves is walking blindly uptown and none of these clowns know who I am. They'll probably lynch some Satanist in Alphabet City."

Tobey twisted his mouth in vague disapproval. "You mean SoHo."

"Fuck, you're right. Just for the alliteration alone."

"Yeah."

"Excuse me, Messrs. Fitzgerald and Hemingway?" Oz interrupted. "These Christians are alarming. I think we should go back to the hotel and get Gladstone out of sight."

"Until when?" I asked.

"Until we know the seriousness of the threat. Jeeves is looking for you. These Christians. Fucking zombies. Who knows who else?"

"That's true," Tobey said. "Could even be an international thing. I mean, if Koreans can celebrate Christmas, who's to say the reach of an Internet Messiah?"

"I can go undercover with the Christians," Oz said, and we looked at her long and hard.

"Well, not dressed like this, obviously. I'll change."

Tobey agreed. "I know somewhere you can buy a Catholic schoolgirl uniform. Follow me!"

"Go undercover with the Christians. What does that even mean?" I asked.

"I dunno, but any information would be more than we have," Oz said. "And maybe I can even meet up with my friend. He might know something. I think he works for the government or something."

Only surprise can make your stomach sick with the weight of something hollow. "Your friend works for the government? As what?"

"Some cog somewhere. I don't know your departments. In Aus, we just do whatever the guy with the most koalas tells us to do."

"Look, I'm all for making fun of Australia, but it doesn't suit you. Especially when you're deflecting. Your mystery buddy's gonna solve all our problems, is he?"

Oz smiled. "Aww, don't be jealous," she said, scratching the stubble under my chin. "He's nothing like you. Just some guy in an office. Not the savior of all e-humanity."

Tobey became the voice of authority. "Gladballs, just get unseen and let Oz and me do some poking around while you update the journal or whatever."

I waited for the pit in my stomach to fill with calming rationalizations.

"Two days," I said. "I don't want to be alone longer than that."

"Done," Oz said.

"Promise you'll come for me in two days."

"I'll come, but will *you* be there when I get there?" Oz asked.

"Where else?"

"I don't know. Just be there."

I kissed Oz good-bye and punched Tobey in the arm before watching them go off. I felt a bit guilty about them facing the unknown, if not danger, while I returned to a room with a bed and a TV. I knew I wasn't a messiah, but, ultimately, hiding was just too unmessiah-y, so I decided to just be careful: avoiding Jeeves uptown and remembering not to say "Hey, I'm the messiah!" to any crusading Christian looking for a crucifixion.

The basement Starbucks at 30 Rock was only a few minutes away, and I took Tobey's advice, spending the next few hours updating my journal while listening to Paul McCartney, Neko Case, and even the Indigo Girls. Romaya used to have some Indigo Girls CDs in her collection, and though not a big fan, she admitted to liking a few songs before I ruined them for her. Sitting on the edge of our bed with my acoustic guitar, I deconstructed what she enjoyed, exposing it for what it was. The 6/8 strums and third harmonies revealed and repeated. I harassed her until she picked letters from A to G, which I rearranged into the chords of simple songs, and strummed in a folk rock waltz, showing her anyone could do it. And I was right. She liked it. And then she felt stupid for liking it and didn't like it anymore. Thinking of it now, it's hard to recall why knowing how to make her happy was something so worthy of ridicule.

The two lattes and giant M&M cookie I devoured all helped obliterate any trace of the noir private eye vibe I'd perfected. I wiped the last of the foam from my lips before realizing I hadn't touched my flask all day. It was just me and the world outside, and these journal pages were the only things creating any structure to my life. My spine, now one with the Starbucks pleather, dictated movement, but I still had no intention of going home, so I kept my profile low by heading to the safest place I knew: the New York Public Library.

Troops were evacuating young lovers and salad-eating secretaries from Bryant Park for yet another terrorist spot check, but I didn't let that distract me. I was already feeling the library's comfort. Maybe it was a comfort that came from eight tons of marble, but it always seemed like something more. The library stood virtually unchanged for 125 years during good times and bad. Unaffected by war or peace, swing jazz, punk, or disco. It was hard to imagine anything could alter it for the future. Probably a naïve thing to say in a city that suffered 9/11, but it felt true. The faint echo of voices and footsteps, the smell of leather and paper, and the rush of cool air all raised that vague feeling to a religiously certain conviction. This is a sanctuary, at least until a renovation no one needs fucks it up.

I spent a fair amount of time just walking the halls until I felt ready to check out a book, and then I realized I'd never done that before. Not in this palace. I wasn't even sure if it was a reference library or what. That wasn't its point, it seemed to me. It was more a monument to learning. A repository for history. Like the Library of Congress in D.C., but closer to a decent slice of pizza. Besides, what book could I possibly check out that would help me find the Internet? So I went to the third-floor reading room to peruse my now-updated journal in the hopes of seeing something I'd missed before.

I was greeted by Milton's familiar quote carved above the door in golden leaf:

A GOOD BOOKE IS THE PRETIOUS LIFE-BLOOD OF
A MAFTER FPIRIT, IMBALM'D AND TREAFUR'D UP
ON PURPOFE TO A LIFE BEYOND LIFE.

And right below that quote, there used to be a sign touting the room's free Internet access. No longer. But the vaulted ceiling of a painted heaven remained, intimidating as much as it inspired. I felt pressure to find a seat quickly. To quit being the gawking spectator and become one of the dozens of people already hard at work. I chose space 117 at the end of a long table, trying to make my chair screech as little as humanly possible along the floor. I failed, and the woman on the opposite side of the table looked up from her copy of *Tender is the Night* with something that could only be called a kind reprimand. In my rush, I'd chosen poorly. She was beautiful, and no one would believe I had picked this chair at random. Instead, I seemed like one of those guys on the subway who cozies up to the one pretty girl on a half-empty train.

"Sorry," I said as non-provocatively as possible.

"It happens," she said with just the slightest trace of an accent, but I wasn't sure. Even her face wasn't completely revealed. Only her thick brown hair and cobalt eyes appeared over the Fitzgerald.

I wanted to say something like, "I didn't know you were so hot when I chose this seat," but I decided it would be best just to sit quietly and smile.

I laid my journal out before me and started at the beginning. Sometimes, I thought I felt her looking at me, but when I'd sneak a peek, she seemed at peace with her novel. Sometimes, she'd ease it toward the table, and I could see her bite her full lower lip in a way I found impossibly arousing. I kept making my way through pages, looking for missed clues almost as intently as I wondered if the rest of her were as effortlessly attractive as her face. After about twenty minutes, she put down her book and leaned forward over the table. I cringed in embarrassment, waiting to be called out for all my impure thoughts.

"I'm sorry," she whispered. "Can I ask you a question?"

A librarian shushed us before I could answer, and I somehow found the nerve to point outside. An invitation to a full-volume conversation.

She smiled and stood, revealing a simple blue summer dress with tiny white polka dots that I followed out of the reading room and into the third-floor hallway.

"So," she said, spinning around and planting her feet. "This is even more awkward with the build-up of a walk, but I have to know: is that your journal there?" she asked, pointing.

"Yes?"

"So let me ask you this," she continued. "In a library filled with millions of books, how narcissistic does someone have to be to sit and read their own work?"

It might have been one of the most cutting things ever said to me, but somehow her beauty and abuse were only empowering. It kept me calm the way speed settles hyperactive kids.

"True," I said. "But my prose is really just fucking sensational."

She did that thing again, disapproving of me in a completely accepting way, and I told a half truth.

"Actually, it's not my journal. It's notes for a case I'm working on."

"You're a private detective?"

"Well, yeah. Why else would I dress like this?"

"Not sure," she said. "Because you're some sort of insufferable hipster douchebag?"

I laughed and she did too, and it felt different from any of the laughs I'd had these last two months. I could feel this one just like I could feel the tile beneath my feet.

"Let me tell you all about it," I said. "Over coffee?"

She blushed a little.

"Maybe, but you sure your wife wouldn't mind?"

She pointed to my left hand, and I looked down to see my wedding ring. I was wearing my wedding ring. Had I really never taken it off? I was wearing my wedding ring. I was standing in the New York Public Library talking to a beautiful woman. There was a slight wind tunnel in the hallway. Her dress had a tiny fray by the hem of her left shin. I was wearing my wedding ring.

"I have to go," I said. "I'm sorry. I'm not married. I have to go."

"Wait," she said. "What? Are you okay?"

"I'm sorry. You're very beautiful." I took a step backward.

"Thank you. I mean, are you okay?"

She leaned forward slightly, and now I could see

over her shoulder. A man was approaching from the hallway behind her in a frighteningly linear fashion. Rowsdower?

"Is he with you?" I asked. "Is this some trick?"

"I don't understand."

"My wife is dead. I have to go. You're very beautiful."

I rushed down the steps along the perimeter of the main entrance and out to Fifth Avenue. My sanctuary had betrayed me, but Rowsdower would not catch me here.

I was hit by a thick humidity rising into rain. New York was wet and gray. A concrete terrarium for me to cut through while escaping to the B a block away. The subway doors closed. The car was air-conditioned. No one knew me, and I was safe. Safe to take a swig from the flask that had somehow gone untouched all day. There was a slight burn and a tingle that settled. I settled with it.

My fingers were tight on my wedding band, twisting it as I wondered why Oz had never mentioned it. True, married men rarely stay out drinking for two months, or maybe Tobey told her what happened with Romaya, but to not even ask? It didn't seem right. And it also didn't make sense that Rowsdower would have anything to do with the library beauty. If he knew where I was, he didn't need an ingénue to ensnare me. And if he knew where I was, I wouldn't have been able to just run away from him. Would I? But it looked like him. What if he had no backup? Maybe he'd gone rogue? Of course, given the breadth of authority offered by the NET Recovery Act, it was hard to imagine what kind of activities would even be considered against government policy.

I needed Oz and Tobey to help talk this through. I also needed a room with a door. And a lock. The hotel was only a few blocks from the Broadway/Lafayette stop, and I took that extra thirty seconds I always need to get my bearings when I'm off New York's midtown grid. No sign of Rowsdower or roving Christians. No zombies. Just a less populated SoHo filled with the city's youngest, thinnest, most unique and indistinguishable New Yorkers, carving out twenty-first-century existences. Being thirty-seven made me invisible, and I got to my room without incident.

Everything was where I'd left it, and I took a certain comfort from the familiarity even if I didn't remember closing the bathroom door in the foyer entrance to the room. I double-locked the door behind me and walked out into the room, placing my grandfather's fedora on the tiny writing desk before falling into bed.

That's when I heard a flush. My heart tried to run to a safer place, but I managed not to make a sound. Whoever was in the bathroom didn't know I was here, and I thought about running past that closed door and out of the room. But then there was the quick rush of water and the squeak of a towel ring. Too close. I waited in the bed with only the cheap bathroom wall between us.

The door opened, and in the reflection of the room's one mirror, I saw Jeeves exit the bathroom. He stood still with his eyes closed and palms out. Then he smiled.

"Aah," he said. "I've been expecting you."

I was pretty sure I could take Jeeves in a fight, but his serenity held some hope. He opened his eyes and then put his hands in the air like a criminal, his gut rounding out from beneath the edge of his rising Rush 2112 shirt.

"May I enter?" he asked, from the foyer.

I didn't answer. I couldn't.

"Please," he said. "I'm sorry about the surprise, but I promise you, I'm not a bad guy."

He saw his words failed to settle me, and he thought for a moment.

"I don't want anything from you, Gladstone. May I come in?"

I pointed to the small chair.

"Thank you," he said, taking his seat. Not since Oz at the peep show had someone looked so happy to see me. I double-checked the bathroom. It was empty.

"I'm alone," he said. "My functionally retarded minions are wandering the Upper West Side, where I left them. Told them the feelings were very strong up there. Half of them are loitering in the lobby of the Trump International Hotel right now."

"Why'd you do that?" I ask.

"Because fuck Trump," Jeeves said.

"No, I mean, why did you mislead them?"

"Because I'm not your enemy. I just wanted to meet you."

I went to the window. No minions. No zombies. No Rowsdower.

"How did you find me?"

"Haven't you heard? I'm psychic. I *felt* you."

I was struck by something I hadn't noticed before. I had been thrown by his atrocious fashion sense and indifference to body consciousness, but seeing him now, in person, I noticed that certain quality political correctness trained me not to associate with being gay, but there it was. Jeeves was a gay psychic librarian prog-rock fan. It was hard to imagine a more sparsely overlapped Venn diagram.

"How do you know my name?" I asked.

Jeeves rolled his eyes. "Again. Psychic. Also, it's all over your room service receipts. Someone's certainly not the keeping-a-tidy-room messiah," he said, gesturing to the mess.

I laughed. Definitely gay. I sat on the corner of the bed, facing him.

"Gladstone. I found you. Alone. If I were gonna help anyone else, they'd be here already."

Jeeves saw me contemplating trust like a remora in the bathtub.

"The government approached me after O'Reilly bought it, but I didn't give them your description."

"No?"

"Turn on the news." He handed me the remote from the desk.

"Oh, I suppose the perfectly relevant news story is going to be on just at this exact moment?"

"Seriously. What part of psychic don't you understand?"

I turned on NY1:

"Authorities have now released a sketch of the so-called 'Internet Messiah.'"

A crude charcoal drawing came onto the screen revealing a picture of a bearded man in a fedora with a nose distinctly longer than mine.

"Wow. You really Jew'd me up there, didn't you?"

Jeeves was pleased. "Yep. Could be half the city."

"You've just bought a lot of headaches for the fine Hasidim of Crown Heights," I said.

Jeeves just shrugged. I didn't think he was psychic, and I knew I wasn't the Internet Messiah—whatever that was—but I also knew I wasn't in danger. And I wasn't alone. Maybe I trusted him because I felt he and I were both on the outside.

"Jeeves," I said, removing my flask. "Could I offer you a drink?"

He got up to unwrap one of the plastic cups from the bathroom, and I poured him two fingers of Jameson from my flask. It wasn't until the second round that I told him I didn't believe he was psychic.

"I have millions of followers," he protested.

"So does Fred."

"Gladstone, it's not 2009. Fred hasn't been relevant for years. You need to update your references."

The Internet had kept Jeeves young, and I could tell he must have devoured social media as hungrily as he consumed books earlier in life. I had too, but he was in his fifties, so it was even more impressive.

"Not that I think getting lucky on O'Reilly and knowing the local news schedule makes you clairvoyant," I said, "but do you mind telling me what the fuck an Internet Messiah even is?"

"It's just a name. You're the guy who brings back the Net. Web Locator? Net Finder? I'm going with Internet Messiah. More of a ring."

"Yeah, but how?"

"Well, if I knew that, I'd be the Internet Messiah, wouldn't I?"

Jeeves had a fair point, and I could see I'd never be able to pin him down. It was something I didn't understand, like gamer-based memes, and I stopped pursuing it. I just let him drink. I drank too.

"What does the government want from me?"

"Whaddya mean? The same thing we all want from you. To bring back the Net."

"Or maybe they're the ones who took it down and they want to *stop* me from bringing it back. Did you ever think of that?"

"I have," Jeeves said. "But does that mean you believe you're actually capable of bringing it back?"

I poured myself another while Jeeves nursed his.

"Yeah, I'm not sure, Gladstone," he said. "I couldn't

feel their motives, I just didn't help them because, y'know, fuck 'em. The Internet is for us."

"Yeah, it's what I had instead of a passport."

"Why don't you have a passport?"

"I don't know. I never got one. I mean, I had no money as a kid. What was the point? And then with the honeymoon, well, we got married in a hurry and there was no money for a European vacation or anything. And then, well, it was just another thing I never did."

I thought of Romaya. How she had bought a passport with her Taco Bell earnings as a teenage girl in Eureka before I ever met her. It expired during our marriage, before she got to go anywhere.

"Well, yeah, the Net made the world smaller," Jeeves said. "But not just distance. It shrinks differences in money, power, influence. I mean, just about everyone had the Net. Everyone could watch the latest YouTube video. Bill Gates and Barack Obama and Warren Buffett have probably all heard of . . ."

Jeeves searched his memory for the most widespread memes of the last few years.

"Two Girls One Cup? Lemon Party?" I offered.

"Those are the first that occurred to you?" he asked. "Christ, Gladstone. Did *you* destroy the Internet just to get rid of your cookies? No. I was gonna say something like LOLcats."

We sat for a while. I opened another bottle I kept in the writing desk. Sometimes, he'd stare at me, trying to figure out how I could be the man he thought I was, but mostly he didn't.

"So," I said after a while. "This not working for a living is pretty great, huh?"

"Fantastic," he said, his words barely escaping his smile. "But, y'know, I work. You've seen me out in the park."

"That's not work."

"You're right. It's not. . . . To not having bosses." He raised his cup.

"Aren't you afraid that will all go away if the Net comes back? You'll lose your niche."

"I'm okay. I'm famous now. The Net comes back, I'll do a podcast or a YouTube channel or something. Write an e-book. I can live out the rest of my life fake-famous and tethered to a PayPal account. Besides, look at me. My needs are few."

"That's true. I guess you'll have more than enough to keep you in ponytail ties and prog-rock concert shirts."

Jeeves checked the time on the TV and rose from his seat. "I should be going. I must gather my minions."

"Aww, can't you sit with me a little longer? One more drink?"

Jeeves looked down at me. There was wonder and concern.

"I'm not sure that's a good idea," he said.

"Not much of a drinker?" I asked.

"I wasn't talking about me."

———

I must have passed out because I woke up the next afternoon on top of the sheets still in my clothes. Jeeves was nowhere to be seen. One bottle was kicked and another was close to joining it. The room, however, still seemed pretty much intact except for a note taped to the door, reading, "Look in your jacket pocket."

My body moved faster than the hangover wanted it to. My head darted around the room for further signs of intrusion, but there were none. Just that note that scared me more than I could understand. I reached into my pocket slowly, relieved to find the comfort of my flask. But when I removed my empty companion, I felt the hard edges of a note, folded and square. I turned away, sensing it from the corner of my eye as I slowly unworked the folds, but it wasn't a threat or a ransom. Just a note from Oz.

> Dear Drinky,
> I couldn't wake you, but I stayed long enough to make sure you didn't choke to death on your vomit, rock star. I'll be back later. Be safe.
> Miss you,
> Oz
> P.S. I haven't found my friend yet, but these Christians are a hoot. Tell you later.

I closed the note and returned it to my pocket where it seemed to belong. My remaining hours alone are a bit cloudy. I remember the longest shower of my life. A liquor store run. Some room service, and not much else.

DAY 57. UNDESIRABLE NO. 1

Something in my dreams smelled wonderful, and it was caring for me. Keeping me warm.

"Wake up, old man."

It was Oz, and she was staring down at me with less than her usual zeal.

"Look in your pocket," she said.

"I got your note, thanks."

"No, not that," she said. "Something else."

"Again with the pocket? Why can't you just hand me things like a normal person?" I asked, and she smiled.

I reached inside and once again unfolded a piece of paper folded in fours. This time it was a flier. A wanted poster. Apparently, I was a person of interest under the NET Recovery Act and wanted for questioning. The faulty sketch from the news stared back at me.

"Seems like you're Undesirable No. 1," she said.

"*Harry Potter* reference?"

Oz shrugged.

"See, I would have gone with *1984* there."

"What, you mean like Goldstein?"

"Well, yeah. I even have a book . . ."

While Oz considered the superiority of my reference, I reached up for assistance and then pulled her down onto the bed with me. Oldest trick in the book.

"For fuck's sake, Gladstone! This isn't a joke."

"Calm down. They don't know who I am and that pic looks nothing like me."

"Yeah, but those Christians . . . They fucking *hate* you. It's not even logical. No one even has the same reason. You're like this inkblot for all their hostility. You took the Net. You created the Net. You want to displace Jesus with the Net. Oh, and my favorite: that you and Jeeves have some sort of sick sex thing."

"Not my type," I said. "He's not even Australian."

I sat up and looked down at Oz laid out before me. Even in an undercover Christian blouse and sensible shorts (I'm guessing Talbots), she was incredibly sexy. I opened her legs and pulled her close to me. The back of her thighs over the top of my legs.

"Tell me what you've learned about Christians Against the Messiah," I said, running my hands inward.

"Well, there's some good news," she said.

"Oh my God," I said. "You embed with Christians for just two days and you're already spreading the good news."

"Ha, very funny, fuckwit."

Her beige shorts might have been loose and Martha Stewart-approved, but that only made it easier for my right hand to slip up and inside. And with the sensible hem now resting up to my forearm, I could tell she wasn't wearing underwear. This was the Oz I was crazy about. Able to put on the enemy's clothing and still deliver an under-the-radar fuck you.

"I'm sorry. Tell me the good news," I said, my thumb running down the length of her and slowly back up. She bit her lip like the woman in the library as I settled into tiny circles.

"You said there was good news, Oz. What's the matter? Can't you tell me?"

I started undoing the shorts with my other hand.

"God, you're the worst," she said. "The good news is that when they released that Jewy sketch of you . . . when they released that sketch, half the Christians took off to find you in Brooklyn."

"But that means they won't be allowed back into the city?"

"Exactly. Half your problem just went away."

That was a call for a celebration. Christians in disarray. Zombies uptown. A government that didn't know my face or name. And a beautiful woman in my bed.

"Hey, can you do me a favor?" I asked, pulling down her shorts.

"Yeah?"

"Can you let me call you Jeeves? It's, like, the *only* way I can even come close to getting an erection these days."

"I hate you so fucking much, Gladstone."

I woke up on the couch. The back of my head dull and flat from the armrest. My neck stiff, and my journal splayed open on my chest. It reminded me of those times I hadn't followed Romaya to bed. When I fell asleep with the laptop on my stomach. Or at least half asleep, after leaving half-considered comments on half-remembered sites for virtual people to halfheartedly read or fully ignore. Oz wasn't in the bed, and I felt that energy in my fingers again until she emerged from the shower in a towel.

"Go clean up," she said. "I told Tobey we'd meet him at one."

"When did you speak to Tobey?"

"Wednesday, when you were in hiding."

"Isn't today Wednesday?"

"Thursday."

"Wow, it's really easy to lose whole days without work to quantize your pain, isn't it?"

Oz filled me in on the details on the way to the East Side. Tobey had picked a diner not too far away from his UN gig so we could compare notes, provided it was safe for me to come out of hiding. And with CAM partially banished and befuddled, it was apparently safe. Now, I'd find out what was going on internationally. Or at least what Tobey thought was going on internationally.

I opened the door for Oz because even post-punk, bad-ass grrls like to be treated like ladies. Tobey was already there, and he greeted us with a smile, gesturing and pulling all the air toward him with an open palm. An easy grace befitting a man presiding over his booth like lord of the manor.

"Are we late?" I asked.

"Not at all. Please. Sit. Let me get you some refreshments."

He shouted out to the waitress, "Madame, some disco fries, a coffee, a Dr Pepper, and your finest dingo juice for my Australian friend here."

The waitress came with the drinks a moment later, correctly surmising that Tobey was the kind of crazy best to quietly patronize.

"This beverage looks remarkably like ginger ale," Oz said, while I sipped half of my coffee to make room for whiskey.

"Well, that's what *we* call it *here*," Tobey said. "But enough about your country's odd nomenclature. So! G-Face. Gotta tell you. Lots of people with lots of money are *very* interested in you."

"Me or the Internet Messiah?"

"Well, that's the same thing, isn't it?

I took one of Tobey's fries. The one with cheese ensnaring four additional fries. It was the least I could do after his nacho shenanigans.

"Where you getting your info, Tobes?"

"Um, how about, the UN? I mean, I *am* a page. I hear things. Then I speak. Then other people hear the things I say. We call that having a conversation. It's technical, but I think I've put together some attractive offers for you."

Oz slammed down her drink, spilling some on the

table. "Tobey, you fuckwit. Have you been blabbing about Gladstone?"

Her voice, which started in a scream, dialed down to a whisper by the sentence's end as she looked around the diner for adversaries. There were some Asians in one booth. Men of Arab extraction in another. Pakistani maybe. Other dudes who could have been Russian. I wasn't sure. It's hard to tell without the furry hats.

"First of all," Tobey said. "If you didn't want the dingo juice you could have just said so. That's just wasteful. And second, how stupid do you think I am? Of course I haven't. I've just made it known that I may or may not have a connection to the Internet Messiah."

"And did it occur to you that you may or may not have given them an incentive to have you followed, bugged, traced, whatever, y'know, just to discover who this Internet Messiah might be that you may or may not know?"

"You're being paranoid."

"Am I?" Oz asked, looking over her shoulder. "I mean, look at this place. Could be anyone."

"Uh, that's because this is New York City. Tell her, Gladstone. They have minorities here. It's not like Australia where everyone looks like Yahoo Serious or the chick with red shoes from the 'Let's Dance' video."

"Are all your Australia references eighties-based?"

"Has anything happened in Australia since the

eighties? I mean, besides Nemo being reunited with his dad?"

"All right, enough," I said. "I think we're safe for the time being. But what do they even want with the Messiah?"

"Are you kidding me? It's the Internet. It's like the new nuke. Everyone wants it. Whatever country first reclaims the Net wields a huge cache of wealth and power."

I guess that was a fair point. We were no closer to knowing who had stolen the Net, but at least we knew all the people who wanted it.

"So," Tobey said, finishing the last of the fries, "in exchange for exclusive control of the Net, a spokesman for Japan has offered the Messiah five hundred million and a lifetime tax-free residence."

"Holy fuck," Oz said. "Wait, dollars or yen?"

"Does it matter?" Tobey asked.

"Well, it is a ten to one ratio. . . ."

We both stared at Oz.

"What? You think only Aussies want to see me shower? A girl's got to know these things. Only a moron would trust PayPal implicitly."

"Fair enough," said Tobey. "Anyway, Germany has also made an almost identical offer. Five hundred million yen, dollars, krauts, whatever."

"That's great and all," I said. "But I'm pretty sure when I took their money and couldn't produce the Net, it would lead to some problems."

"I think you should listen to all the offers before forming any opinions," Tobey insisted.

"Well, aren't they all pretty much the same? The Net for money?"

"Not so fast. Saudi Arabia has also promised not only 'countless riches,' but also twenty-four/seven military protection from those 'who would see the streets run red with the Messiah's Zionist blood.'"

"Man, that was one Jewy sketch," I said.

"The Jewiest."

"More like Nazi art therapy," Oz offered.

"Speaking of hate," Tobey said, "I'm sorry to report there were no offers from Australia."

"Guess they couldn't spare any Bloomin Onions," I said.

"Crikey." Tobey nodded. "Did I do that right, Oz? 'Crikey' means many things, like how you can use 'Smurf' in lots of ways, right?"

"Yes. Like in this case it means the speaker is a nipple-dicked American d-bag."

"Okay, kids," I said. "Enough fun. What now?"

"Well, I'd go live in Japan," Tobes suggested. "Not that Germany isn't tempting, but, I dunno, Japan's women are just hotter, on average."

Tobey smiled the smile of a man fully aware of how annoying he was being. But then I saw it turn to concern. Fear. I turned to face whatever he was seeing over my shoulder that made him so afraid. I saw one of the Arabs coming down at me with a steak knife just in time to catch his wrist an inch before impact. His two buddies flashed by the corner of my eye, no doubt occupying Oz and Tobey, who were noticeably absent from my struggle as the blade, shaking by my left ear, angled toward my jugular.

It wasn't a graceful fight. He was standing, and I was kneeling on the squishy cushion of the diner booth. But he no longer had the element of surprise. If I could just stand on the seat before he drove the serrated knife into me, he'd lose his leverage too. He was about fifty, greasy, graying, and filled with a child's anger. He was also clearly right-hand dominant, and overtaking my left. I could feel the knife against my skin as my left knee sunk deeper into the booth. I stretched my right leg out to the side, feeling for the hard vinyl corner. I found it just as he smiled, seeing the knife draw first blood, but not knowing he'd already lost.

I sprung forward over the booth and into his chest. When we landed, I was on top of him and the knife was on the floor. I brought a wicked right cross against his face. The kind of punch I'd always imagined and never thrown. And after it connected, I drove my knees into his arms.

"Why are you trying to kill me?" I screamed down with full force. The blow had drained his power, but not his hatred.

"Your journal," he growled.

My first question should have been how this random man had even heard of my journal, but for reasons I'm still not sure of, that thought didn't occur to me. Maybe it was all the Messiah talk or Oz's fear that each of these diner patrons hid some international agenda, but in that moment all I could think of was that he believed my journal held the answer to the Internet mystery. That I was the Messiah.

"My book won't tell you anything! It's nothing."

"It is an insult! It is filled with lies!"

I had no idea what he meant.

"Why do you describe the smut peddlers as 'smiling Pakistanis'?"

"What?"

"In your filthy book of lies. Your journal. Why do you make the porn sellers Pakistani? I am Pakistani. Am I a pornographer?"

The suited Japanese were pointing and conferring. Two Saudi Arabian men I hadn't noticed before removed their sunglasses and stood from their booth. Even the Russians were engaged.

"You read my book? But how did—"

I felt a hand on my shoulder. It was Oz. Tobey was already outside pretending not to know me. I looked over my shoulder at our empty booth. No trace of the other Arabs.

"You about good to go, chief?" she asked.

The mini UN of Third Avenue diner patrons was now all in a row, staring at the international incident on the floor. Whether they thought I was a messiah or a lunatic holding down a beaten busboy was impossible to tell, but I knew it wasn't safe either way.

"Excuse us," Oz said to the crowd. "We have to um . . . fuck off. Now."

Internet People

I may have been drunk and scared, but I could see the cycles. The signs of trouble, the flight, the subway providing escape. It was getting old. Unsustainable. Still, the three of us took comfort in motion and closed doors. Feeling the confines of your immediate universe like an embrace while still knowing nothing can catch you as long as you don't stop moving between two worlds. The feeling didn't last.

"The fuck was that, Gladstone?" Oz demanded.

"I have no idea. Apparently, Pakistan would rather kill me than make use of my alleged messianic prowess."

"Uh, yeah, either that or you're a psychotic busboy murderer," Tobey said.

"What? He attacked me! You saw."

Tobey was slow to respond. He was choosing his words. Something I'd never seen him do before. And when he looked up from the floor he looked at Oz before turning to me. Another first.

"Well, I did see a busboy drop a whole plate of dishes just behind you . . . but then it looked like you just beat the living shit out of him."

"Yeah, I get that way when people pull a knife on

me. My back was to you. Probably blocking the whole thing."

They were not impressed.

"What about all the stares of the mini UN, eyeing me like fresh meat? You miss that too?"

"Well, yeah, that I saw," Oz said. "Which is why I called Tobey a twit in the first place, and why I got us out of there."

"Thank you!"

"But," Oz continued. "Maybe they were all looking at the lunatic who was beating the fuck out of a busboy."

"He attacked me!"

"Why?" Tobey asked.

I started to answer, realizing none of the words made sense, but also knowing there was no turning back now. "He said it was because I'd insulted Pakistanis in my journal."

"How'd he read your journal? That's retarded."

"I know! But none of this makes sense, and I'm sick of it. Zombies and Christian zealots and now the foreign governments."

"Well, the foreign governments only want to give you money, so I'm not sure what you're complaining about."

"Again. Not the Internet Messiah."

"How do you know?" Tobey asked.

"What?"

Tobey got off his seat, taking a spot in front of Oz and me with a wide stance. It helped him keep his

balance on the rocking of the downtown 6, but it also
let him put his face even with ours when he leaned
forward. He spoke close and quiet. "Jeeves says you
are. Anonymous believes in you. Strangers seem compelled to follow you. When we were separated, you
found Oz and me. . . ."

Tobey watched me consider his words.

"Not to mention," he added, sweetening the pot,
"your mom popped you out in a manger after getting
fucked by God. . . ."

"Well, that's a fair point. . . ."

Oz moved inward with an intense agitation. "Fuck
it. Tobes is right," she said. "Who are we to doubt
Jeeves? I decided to put my lot in with you instantly."

"So let me get this straight," I said. "First, the two
of you think I'm violent and batshit insane, and now
I'm the Messiah."

"Well, more of a fiery Old Testament messiah," Tobey said. "But yeah, who says the Messiah's not nuts?"

Now it was my turn to stand. I assumed a stance
not too different from Tobey's and he took my seat
next to Oz. I was going to work through this like a
lecturing professor.

"Okay. Fine," I said. "Let's go with that. I'm the
Messiah. So . . . what? You want me to field offers
from foreign governments? Seriously?"

Oz spoke before Tobey could. "Or, y'know, you could
just work for this one. I'm sure they'd make it worth
your while and you wouldn't even have to pack."

"What?"

"What do you mean 'what'?" she asked, suddenly seeming very small, like any other person.

"I mean what are you talking about? Work for the government. Fuck the government and their NET Recovery Act bullshit. Who even knows what they're up to? Or if they're even the ones who took the Net away."

"Well that would be one way to find out, right?"

"No. Not right, and more importantly, fuck you. When did you become my recruiter? I'm not looking for a job. I'm off the grid. Free. The disability payments keep me alive, and I answer to no one. All I have to do is nothing."

"Y'know," Tobey said. "Most people hate their job. You know that, right?"

"Are you fucking kidding me? You think you know what a job is? You blog for a living. You work in your boxers, cruising news reports you can add blowjob jokes to, and then scrape the ad revenue for rent. You're gonna talk to me about work?"

"Easy, Gladstone," Oz said.

"No, I'm not going to take it easy. You were so disgusted by the notion of a job you let strangers watch you shower for money. Congratulations. Well, unlike you, I put in my time, and I'm fucking done."

Tobey and Oz did not reply. They did not look at me, but there did seem to be some sort of unspoken understanding between them.

"Wait a minute," I said. "You go to work for the UN and now suddenly me cooperating with foreign governments is a good idea?"

"Look, I'm just—"

"Shut up, Tobey," I said, and turned to Oz. "And you. You go visit your friend. Your little friend who works for the government, the one you came to New York to meet in the first place, and suddenly I should go to work for the government? Who is this guy?"

"I never met up with him. I can't find him."

"Right."

"I don't know what happened to him!" she insisted.

"I don't even know who you are. I can't trust you. You're not real. Either of you. Fucking Internet people."

They didn't move for fear of scratching up against the sharp ugly words I had put into the world. And I didn't move either, realizing I might not have escaped the enemy after all. So we sat tight for the moment, feeling the rumble of the tracks. Oz put her pain only partially on display. Hiding the ancient scars while flaunting the fresh wounds I'd just inflicted. Tobey feigned indifference and started rolling a joint in plain sight as the doors opened on Bleecker Street.

"Fuck this," I said, and jumped out onto the platform before they closed again.

Oz rushed to the doors, now closed, slapping against the glass and saying something I could not hear. She started to cry as the train took her away.

11.

DAY 57. HAMILTON BURKE

A whole life in New York and I still can't navigate the Village. I'm useless south of the city's right-angle grid, and I really didn't feel like getting lost, so I just walked south. I'd hit the water eventually, and then there'd be nowhere else to go.

I sat on a seaport bench for hours, drinking and watching the boats go nowhere. I killed the Jameson within an hour, but I didn't move. Not even after the sun set. Not until my nerves cut through the fog of liquor and darkness, demanding motion to distribute the energy. The financial district had gone home. It was always dead at night, stockbrokers having left for the day, but in the Apocalypse it was especially dead. More than half the city was now simply gone all the time. Many were tired of waiting for the one terrorist threat that turned out to be true. Some were just tired of the warnings. Even the mosquitoes that don't bite can drive you away.

I tried to enjoy the surreal calm of being completely alone in New York, suppressing the nagging thought that perhaps a bomb had dropped while I wasn't paying attention or that I was already dead. I passed the charging bull at Bowling Green Park and then meandered back to Wall Street before taking it up all the way to Broadway. The towering cross of Trinity Church guided my way, framed in the sky by the hard lines of Wall Street's rooftops. So overt you'd call it forced perspective if it weren't real.

A few cabs passed when I got to Broadway, breaking the silence. I crossed and headed down Rector along the iron spiked fence of Trinity's courtyard. Someone was on the sidewalk staring inward. The silhouette of an older man: bald, stout, and, upon closer inspection, wearing a three-piece suit. Something of an accomplishment in a New York summer.

As I got closer, I grew more excited, because I knew exactly what had captured his attention: Alexander Hamilton's grave. It was impossible to believe that one of our founding fathers was close enough to throw a rock at. Just ten feet through a fence on a tiny side street unwatched by police or soldiers. Hell, during the day, you could even enter the courtyard and touch the thing. An impressive stone monument in the back-yard of a two-hundred-year-old church, now overlooking a cobbler's store the size of a closet and a place for truly mediocre bagels. The architect of America's economy was resting in peace just a block from a C-minus strip club once known for five dollar handjobs.

"Hamilton?" I asked.

He looked surprised. "Oh, Alexander Hamilton. Yes," he said, returning his gaze to the headstone.

I stood by his side and stared along with him. Robert Fulton was one plot over competing for attention, but only Hamilton's grave stirred our imagination.

"This is one of my favorite parts of the city," he said.

"Mine too. I mean, the monument to Washington down the street is great. It's cool to think that's where he took his oath, but this *is* Alexander Hamilton. Right *here*."

"I come here sometimes," he said. "Think about things. Think about what he would have thought about things."

I nodded in agreement, although I knew already this man's connection to Hamilton went beyond my love for preserved antiquity.

"Are you a stockbroker, Mr . . ."

"Gladstone. No. No I'm not."

"Ah, me neither. I'm retired. Met quite a few though. I'm Hamilton Burke," he said, extending his hand.

"Hamilton?"

"Yeah, that's my namesake." He pointed to the grave, and took off his steel-rimmed glasses before cleaning them on his red silk tie.

"He founded the Bank of New York, y'know."

"I do," I said.

"So what kind of work do you do, Mr. Gladstone?"

"Well, to tell you the truth, Mr. Burke, right now, nothing. I'm on disability."

"You seem able-bodied enough. I'm sorry if that's too personal. . . ."

"I am, it's just . . . well, it's complicated."

His frown was almost discernible, and I felt the need to break it before it became undeniable.

"What are you contemplating with Mr. Hamilton's help tonight?" I asked.

He smiled and removed a cigar from inside his pocket. "Well, that's complicated too." He clipped the end with an elegant device he took from his front vest pocket. "Cigar?"

I refused, but removed my flask so I wasn't the only one without a friend. "I'm sorry I don't have a glass to offer you. . . ."

"Oh, that's okay. I have my own. And mine's filled with Beauté de Siècle by Hennessy."

That was probably a good thing, considering my flask was kicked. He placed the cigar between his teeth while he unscrewed his flask. Then he poured some of the brandy into the cap.

"Would you hold this for a moment?" he asked, handing me the flask. Then he took the cut end of his cigar and dipped it into the brandy cap, letting the leaves soak up the alcohol.

"I guess I'm thinking about this Internet Apocalypse. And, of course, its effect on business."

He accented his words with a flame that flowed from maybe the nicest lighter I'd ever seen, and it was hard to believe that something as elegant as the ritual being performed before me could make you die in tremendous pain, consumed from the inside out. I'd never wanted a cigar more, but I took my swig, pretending my flask was still filled and all I needed.

"I have to tell you, Mr. Burke. I've been thinking about that too. Even conducting a little investigation with my time off. Y'know, in my own small way."

For the first time, his attention was fully on me, and the former Secretary of the Treasury became just some bones in the ground.

"Really, and what have you found?"

"Not an awful lot, I'm afraid."

The frown I'd preempted before now returned twofold and suddenly his cigar grew distasteful to him. "Dominicans," he said, and tossed it in the street behind him. "You'd think I'd learn by now."

I shrugged, not knowing what to say.

"So, what was your business before becoming an ineffectual detective?"

"I was a claims manager for the New York Workers' Compensation Board, and I'm sorry you're not impressed with my investigation. I'll reduce the rates I'm charging you immediately."

He laughed. "Fair enough," he said. "I guess I sound

like some Internet commenter complaining about the quality of free content."

That was not a reference I was expecting. "You know a lot about that, do you?"

"The Internet? Well, why not? I had to figure out how to monetize that just like everything else."

I could tell I was dealing with another adult who had a job I didn't understand, and if I didn't get it now I knew I never would. When I was a little kid, I pretty much thought there were only six jobs in the world: doctor, lawyer, teacher, fireman, policeman, and astronaut. The rest were a blur of things I never took the time to know.

"Did you enjoy your work, Mr. Gladstone?" he asked pulling another cigar from a different pocket.

I couldn't help staring at the replacement.

"Oh, don't worry," he said. "This one's a Cuban. You were supposed to smoke the Macanudo."

He had not even the slightest trace of embarrassment admitting the inequity of his generosity, and this time, he lit up without the assistance of brandy. Apparently Cubans didn't require such a boost.

"No, sir. I did not enjoy my work."

"And why is that?"

"Well, I was studying to be a lawyer, but my wife and I got pregnant so I took the claims job."

"Oh, I see." He nodded and pulled his face down at the corners in faux consideration. "And do you think you would have liked being a lawyer?"

"No. I'm pretty sure I would have hated that too."

"And why is that?" He seemed to know the answer already.

"Well, in theory, the gig's okay. I liked torts. The human story behind the injury, the analysis of fault, the concepts of compensation. Somewhat engaging in a vacuum, but when you put it in practice . . ."

I paused, looking for the right words.

"The business gets in the way?"

That was about as elegant a description of the problem as I'd ever heard, and Hamilton had nearly suffered an aneurysm waiting for me to get to the point where he could drop that gem.

"Yes. The business gets in the way."

He smiled and exhaled up into the New York City night. The cloud dissipated as it wafted toward the grave.

"Mr. Gladstone, I know it might be hard for a twenty-first-century man under forty to believe, but you are not special. Your story is common, and I guess I was just lucky. Somehow, at a very early age, I realized that at the heart of every occupation, every job, every identity is business. Very few people can procure an existence devoid of business. So why not cut out the middle man? I decided to be in the business of business. I made money for a living."

"Well, I guess you're truly blessed. And this knowledge made you happy?"

"Happy? Oh, I don't know. But I can tell you I was never unhappy because I wanted something I couldn't have. I was never unhappy because I could not give my children the enjoyments and opportunities I thought they deserved. I was never unhappy because my existence was in the control of another man. That's the kind of unhappiness that makes men crawl inside bottles. Put shotguns in their mouths. I've dodged those bullets, but a deeper happiness? It's hard to say. Were you happy with your choices?"

"I told you I wasn't. And I would think a man as successful as you would have learned it's bad form to gloat."

"I apologize. If it makes you feel better, it's not all your fault. It's a rigged game. And the Internet was behind your misery as much as anything else."

I may not have amassed Hamilton's fortune, but I was smart enough to know that the best way to get him talking was not to speak. I placed my flask inside my coat pocket and gave him my full attention.

"Alfred Nobel," he said. "The peace prize guy. Know what he invented?"

"Yeah. Dynamite."

"Correct! They thought it would end war. That big violent explosion. Who would subject their troops to such a creation? They said the same thing about the machine gun. And the nuclear bomb. But man has never invented a weapon he failed to use. You can see where I'm going with this. . . ."

"Y'know, Mr. Burke. I think I will take one of those cigars. A Cuban. If you've got it. Y'know, to give me something to do while you're schooling me."

He took out another cigar, even cutting and lighting it for me. After three puffs I could almost see the chemicals dancing on my tongue.

"There has not been a piece of technology designed to save labor that has not increased labor," Burke said. "Word processors allow you to do what your secretary used to do for you. The Internet, BlackBerries, iPhones, yes they keep you tethered, but that's not the main problem. It's that along with increasing personal productivity, they increase the expectation of productivity. It no longer becomes a bonus to do the work of one and a half men, but the norm. And then when everyone's working at one hundred and fifty percent capacity, they can fire a third of the workforce and still maintain output."

Perhaps it was the hours of drinking or the way the Cuban had escalated the chemical reactions, but I took out my journal to take notes. I'm still not sure if I was trying to mock him or actually learn something.

"You cannot change business. Business is a maniac in a hockey mask. In 1920, an anarchist exploded a bomb in a horse-drawn carriage two blocks from where we're standing. Right in front of the House of Morgan. He killed thirty-eight. He injured four hundred. There's still the shrapnel marks in the side of the building. But what did he change? Nothing. You can't tame business. Only remove some of its tools for mayhem. Monopolies were one tool. The Internet was another."

Hamilton stared at my pen flashing across paper.

"So you're a reporter now?" he asked.

"Don't mind me," I said. "All for the investigation."

"The one that's not going so well?"

"Well, I wouldn't say that."

"But you did say that."

"Maybe some of us are modest?"

He laughed. That would have been a good time for me to stop speaking. But I didn't and now I can't write this without cringing because I did something I wouldn't have normally done. And it wasn't the smoke or the liquor. It was the proximity to success. It was the unbearable reflection of my failure in his eyes.

"Right now, there are thousands, maybe millions, who are looking for the Internet Messiah," I said.

"Yes, I am aware of that." Then an unbridled joy broke out across his face. "Mr. Gladstone, are you saying that person is you?"

"Don't be silly, Mr. Burke. I'm just someone who never understood the business of the world the way you did. An ineffectual detective out on disability. Someone who's made too many unhappy choices. But thank you for the cigar and the company. It was a pleasure to meet you."

"Likewise," he said while inspecting me like a new commodity on the exchange. "I hope we speak again."

I put two fingers to the brim of my hat and walked back toward Broadway.

"Mr. Gladstone," he called out while his words

could still reach me. "Forget about past misfortunes. Is the Net what you must find to be happy?"

Fortunately, a truck hit a pothole on Broadway and Wall, and I kept on walking as if I hadn't heard every word.

Return to 4Chan

I walked as fast as I could, pretending my speed was more than just flight from Hamilton. I wanted to believe I was racing toward success. But I was all alone and there wasn't a single person to help or hide me. The only place I'd learned something even close to useful had been at the Bowery Poetry Club, so that's where I headed. It was even Thursday night. Perhaps I could find Anonymous there still integrated and apart from the mindless 4Chan rabble.

And while a destination quickened my pace, I had to hold up when I hit the Bowery. A group of ten CAM members were marching in two rows of five, looking for the Messiah and stopping only occasionally to spit at perceived homosexuals. Some zombies were also milling about on corners, but most of them were mellower these days, having come down from their antsy Net cravings with ever-increasing amounts of weed. I only had to wait a minute for a clearing before I headed for the door. Once again, white shopping bag guy was holding his clipboard.

"Sup, newfag? You sure you're in the right place?" he asked through his poorly cut mouth hole.

"Fuck off, pedo."

I handed him a five and headed inside. The party was a bit thinner than last time, but already in effect. Some dude in a cheap Guy Fawkes mask was clicking through his projected PowerPoint presentation of new memes he'd created. They were all just still images he'd snapped off his TV with boldfaced writing super-imposed via MS Paint. I didn't get a single one. Of course, I wasn't paying much attention either. Just sipping my Jameson at the bar and scanning the room for Quiffmonster42 or any other possible Anonymous members amid a sea of 4Chan pranksters.

Some dude drinking a vodka and cranberry next to me poked me on the shoulder.

"Hey, you wanna see, like, the dirtiest porno ever?" he asked, pointing to his open laptop on the bar. There was a big red X through the Wi-Fi icon in the bottom right corner.

"Not really." I punctuated with a tilt of my head that killed my drink.

"Oh, come on! It's like super dirty. Just press play."

He'd already lined the arrow up on the Windows Media Player PLAY key. I begrudgingly tapped the touchpad.

Within a moment, the video for Rick Astley's "Never Gonna Give You Up" blared out from his computer's shitty little speakers, still audible over his forced laughter.

"You like Rick Astley?" he asked. "Super gay."

"Yes," I said. "I'm super gay for Rick Astley. So gay that I ripped his video to a laptop before the Apocalypse even happened. So I could own it. Oh wait, this is *your* laptop."

He stopped laughing long enough to say, "Shut up, fag. You're the one who pushed play!"

"Guilty. You totally got me," I said. "And now that I'm so pwn'd, could you do me a favor? Could you tell me where to find Quiffmonster42?"

"What makes you think Quiffmonster42 will see *you*?"

"We had a chat a month ago. I'm Gladstone. I'm looking for the Internet."

His face lit up. "Oh, I remember you! I'm Sergeant Turd!" he said. "I stole your jacket and hat."

He stretched out his hand for a shake without a trace of embarrassment. Unfortunately, the death of the Internet had not given rise to the concept of shame.

"Nice to meet you," I said. "So any idea where I might find him?"

"Sorry, Gladstone. He hasn't been here for weeks. Or any of the bigwigs. We think the Feds picked them up."

"Wait, seriously? How do you know?"

"Know? I don't know. Just what I heard. What proof were you looking for? A Wikipedia page?"

Just then, black-suited troops crashed through the doors with weapons drawn.

"Everybody listen up!" the lead soldier screamed.

"I want all former members of the 4Chan /b/forums on the floor!"

A few guys hit the decks, but one guy with an Elvis half mask raised his hand. "I've visited 4Chan, but I never went in the /b/boards. Can I leave?"

"Shut up," one of the Guy Fawkes guys screamed from the back. "Rule number one: don't mention the /b/boards!"

"That's just during raids, newfag," another Guy Fawkes guy corrected.

"This is a fucking raid, you idiot," came the reply just before the two descended on each other in an absurd slap fight that sent tables and chairs flying— mostly by the crowd that gathered to root and cheer.

In the confusion, I ran for the back room Quiff had shown me last time. I didn't turn to see if anyone noticed, but I could hear the sounds of marching boots and strict military orders: "on the floor," "no one move," "hold still, /b/tards!" Even in my fear, I had to smile when someone taunted, "You mad, bro?"

I made it to the back room. The same shitty couch and closet I'd remembered from before, but the room was empty. No 4Chan royalty. No assistance to be found. And the soldiers were still coming.

The closet opened, revealing that same middle-aged fat man in a Nixon mask from the time before. Once again, naked, but this time not covered in hentai porn and ejaculate.

"Gladstone, get in here," he said.

"Um, Glendoria was it?"

"Glendoria4, yeah. They're coming. Get in. I can hide you."

"Um . . ."

"Trust me, Gladstone. Getting felt up by a perv is the least of your worries now."

It wasn't that I trusted Glendoria4, but I had nowhere else to go. The boots were only getting louder. I got in the closet.

"Listen, Gladstone. Before they took Quiff, he readied this closet. There's a false wall that leads out to a crawl space. Follow the space until it drops down to the boiler room and then take the emergency exit out to the alley."

I could hear the soldiers tearing up the place.

"Go now," Glendoria4 said. "I'll distract them."

I worked my way to the back of the closet and felt for an edge. Glendoria4 was right. Half the back wall was just sliced drywall held in place with a duct tape seam. Not quite Batcave stuff, but, again, not sure what I was expecting.

"I saw him come in here," one of the soldiers said.

I exited just as I heard someone say "check the closet," and listened from the other side of the false wall as I smoothed another piece of duct tape from the other side. That's when I heard the surprise and disgust that could have only been born by Glendoria4 doing his patented falling-out-of-the-closet-while-masturbating move. You really couldn't ask for a better distraction. I made my way down the crawl space, down to the boiler room, and out the emergency exit, all like Glendoria4 had said. Somehow, I had escaped the soldiers even if I had nowhere else to go. Even if I was still completely offline and alone.

I headed to the hotel as slowly and secretly as I knew how. It was late and I was so tired. But still, from the alley across the street, I watched people go in and out of the hotel for over an hour. When even a hipster douchebag with a fedora didn't get stopped, I was pretty confident there was no surveillance going on. I made my way inside and up to my room, but I listened at the door before entering. I wasn't sure if Oz and Tobey were inside and, if they were, if they could be trusted. I couldn't hear anything. I opened the door slowly to peek.

Oz was alone and upset. Her hand against the window, looking down at the street below. She looked up. Her ghostly reflection stared back at me from the glass. She'd been crying.

"You left me," she said.

I remember coming home early one night to check on Romaya. It had been a few days since the third miscarriage and she still hadn't gone back to her copywriting job. I wanted to tell her all the things she'd already heard, all the things I'd already told her. That we would have a child. That someday the setbacks would be far away. But even I felt something dark growing.

The first baby had been an accident and it left almost as quickly as it came. Had Romaya gone another week without pissing on that stick, she wouldn't have even known she was pregnant. But these were different. We were married now. We were in love and a child seemed absolutely necessary. Not because it was expected or because we loved kids. It was more about how much we loved each other. She couldn't let me sleep, and I'd follow her around everywhere when I was awake. That's what the cool people who mock breeders don't understand: that there can be a love bigger than two people. And it swells and spills when you're together. We wanted a baby to share it because not having a child seemed wasteful.

But when a baby wouldn't grow, it made us doubt everything. Our logic was a poor defense against the crazy without shape or order. So I came home, hoping to surprise Romaya with something to make her smile. I didn't have much of a plan. I could hear Peter Gabriel's "I Grieve" coming from the living room as I opened our apartment door, and I stared around the corridor to see her still in her white silk nightgown dancing in our living room. Swaying and spinning like a ballerina angel, the soft fabric of her gown flowing behind, following her motions. Quick and sudden. Erratic, if not so graceful. And though her body moved in long fluid glides, I was struck by her arms, which stayed folded at her chest. I expected exaggerated sweeps and points, but she held them tight.

And then I realized she was holding our baby. Our baby that was never born, but in the still of her arms, it could not have been more real, and she spun and spun and swayed and never let it go. And no matter how tightly she held her arms, the emptiness could not contain all the love that poured out from her.

I must have passed out before even arguing with Oz because I woke up a few hours later on the floor. Oz was no longer crying, and now Tobey was here too.

"I'm not your enemy," she said. "You ass."

"Me either, G-Balls. We're just trying to figure this shit out, y'know?"

I sat up in bed, my head hurting in a way I wasn't used to.

"I overreacted, maybe," I said. "But still. Fuck you, y'know?"

Tobey spoke for both of them. "I get it," he said. "And you're right. Fuck the government. All governments. We'll find it for us."

I nodded my head because I was too tired to speak. Also because I knew this wasn't right. It wasn't real. Something had been broken, and it wouldn't fully heal without a lot of work and time. Work I couldn't do. Time I didn't have.

"We can hit the streets first thing in the morning," Tobey said.

"Yeah, well about that. It might be hard to do without interruption. Y'know, the Messiah business and all."

"What's the problem?" Tobey asked. "Jeeves has

got the zombies uptown, the Christians are fractured, and no one knows what the Messiah looks like."

"Well, in addition to your foreign government shenanigans, I may or may not have been shooting my mouth off tonight about being the Internet Messiah."

"You didn't," Oz said.

"Yeah, I totally did. And then I went to 4Chan, and it coincidentally got raided, so y'know, tomorrow's adventures in New York could be a bit dicey."

Tobey stood. He had that look he got before thinking of a new humorous way to describe how much he wanted to fuck Demi Moore.

"Maybe we don't need to be in New York. Why not try Staten Island!"

"Because we're looking for the Internet, not Italians."

Tobey frowned at my quip. I'd never seen him so serious. "Didn't Quiffmonster42 say Anonymous believed the Internet signals might be coming from Staten Island?"

"Yeah, but if we leave New York, we won't be able to get back," I said.

"But the odds of continuing our search in New York without being spotted are getting slimmer anyway," Tobey said. "Even if you're not the Messiah, everyone's acting like it. Might as well play the part. So whaddya think? Is the Internet in Staten Island?"

I didn't know. I had no intuition. No divine voice leading me. I looked to Oz.

"I don't care," she said. "Just don't ever leave me again. It took me so long to find you."

"I won't."

"Promise."

"Promise," I said.

In the morning, we gathered everything we had, knowing we'd never be coming back. "Maybe we should ditch some of this stuff," I said. "I kinda feel like all these supplies just bog us down."

"We will do no such thing," Tobey said. "We bought this stuff for a reason and we're keeping it."

I couldn't imagine a scenario where we'd need our absurd Kmart camping supplies, but I deferred to the certainty of Tobey's conviction.

"But, maybe you should lose the fedora," he said. "I mean, you're wearing it in that police sketch."

"Yeah, but the sketch is shit, and also if I wear it I can pull it down to obscure the rest of my face anyway."

"True," Tobey said, "but if you take it off, you won't look like a hipster douchebag."

"I'm keeping the hat, Tobes."

Tobey decided to cut his losses arguing with me and turned to the locked bathroom door. "Well, at least you're working the rack today, right Oz?" he called.

Oz emerged from the bathroom in a t-shirt, jeans, and plain brown walking shoes.

"What the fuck is that? Are we going to Staten Island or an Ani DiFranco concert?"

"Sorry, Tobes," she said, "but today's about functionality. I'm not flashing tits on a ferry."

We checked the news before leaving, just to see if there was any last minute information that could affect our journey. The now familiar buzz of NY1 would have been comforting, except it was pretty clear things had gotten worse—a live press conference from City Hall with all the trappings: a podium, suits, and flashing cameras. But most of all, Jeeves.

Apparently, he was now also a person of interest and helping the government in their search. He stood to the side of the podium, visibly uncomfortable by the company he was keeping and the ill-fitting suit he'd been persuaded to wear. It was a gray double-breasted affair, and with his face cleanly shaven and the remnants of his hair pulled tightly back, he looked like Kingpin's weasely kid brother.

I didn't hate him. I didn't feel betrayed or lied to. I knew they had gotten to him. Maybe it was family or a loved one. I wasn't sure, but I felt he'd succumbed to a threat and not a bribe, and I just hoped he was still on my side as much as he could be. My bigger concern was now at the podium. Agent Rowsdower was back, looking leaner than I'd remembered, his skin pulled taut like the yellowed plastic of a laminated skull.

"Good morning, ladies and gentlemen of the press," he said, taking an extra moment to savor the room's collective anticipation. "With the assistance of Mr.

Dan B. McCall here, and based on information obtained from the government's own investigations, we believe we have uncovered the identity of the so-called Internet Messiah."

Everything in my body tightened and suddenly seemed to serve its biological purpose. I could feel the tendons in my arms holding muscle to bone. My veins were filled and flowing. Even the convolutions of my brain quivered like some twisted creature curled up for warmth.

"We believe the Internet Messiah is still in New York and goes by the name Gladstone. He has been declared a person of interest under the NET Recovery Act. The government seeks your assistance in locating him."

I lifted my backpack and headed for the door. "We have to leave now. They'll trace my credit card to the room if they haven't already."

"Easy," Tobey said. "There's no Internet. The hotel has to submit carbons to get paid."

"No, wait." Oz said. "There was still electronic credit card clearance before the Internet."

"Was there?"

"Yeah. Remember in *Say Anything*? The dad's credit card gets turned down at the luggage store. And that was like 1989."

"Yeah, but how? Oh, wait, did it work through the phone lines?"

"I don't care!" I screamed. "Staten Island Ferry. Now!"

No soldiers were waiting for us in the lobby, so we walked north looking for signs of trouble. By the time we got to the turnstiles at Fourteenth Street, we found it: troops spot-checking commuters.

"Quick, take off the fedora," Tobey said.

"Fuck off, Tobey."

"No, I mean, we'll swap hats and I'll wear your sports jacket."

I stopped for a second and tried to consider the possibility of Tobey having a good idea. He did. And it had nothing to do with conning barely legal chicks into flashing their tits. I was impressed, and donned his baseball cap with a smile.

"Maybe I'll even create a diversion. Make them think I'm you," he said, slipping into my sports jacket and limping toward the entrance.

Oz laughed.

"What the hell is that? I don't limp."

"Shush. You're interfering with my process."

Oz scratched at the scruff under my chin the way Romaya used to. "It's okay, Babe," she said. "Let Tobey work his magic."

Then she walked off behind him, still mustering a whole lot of sexuality out of a simple t-shirt and jeans. Two troops instantly asked Tobey to step to the side while a third turned his full supervisory prowess onto Oz's ass. I headed through the turnstiles without a glance and watched them from the platform. One of the troops held the artist's rendering of me next to Tobey and instantly saw that his gene pool was clearly restricted. My friends joined me just in time to catch the train to South Ferry.

South Ferry terminal sprawled out before us, all steel and glass against a clear June sky, and I realized this was the happiest I'd been since the Net died. Longer. The terminal's big majestic letters were more suited to an amusement park ride than a mode of transportation, but that was just as well because the ferry was always the epitome of New York's "no-money-fun." When we were in college, Romaya and I rode the Ferry almost weekly, getting a mini-cruise with a view of lower Manhattan and the Statue of Liberty all for the accommodating price of nothing.

"I want to go inside," she said.

"One day we will. When we have money and time."

One day we did have those things, but it still didn't happen. And then she was gone. And the statue closed. And now, in this Apocalypse, nothing goes to this tiny island.

We found our seats out on the deck beside a man buried in his *New York Times.* Oz closed her eyes to concentrate on the mist hitting her face, and I tried not to stare too hard or to let her see Romaya reflected in my eyes. Tobey seemed happy to have his baseball cap back, and the two of them flanked me on each side, protecting me from the world that wanted more than I could give. A twenty-four-year-old Aussie webcam girl, a twenty-nine-year-old pop-culture blogger, and a thirty-seven-year-old office cog on disability sitting in a row. It was one of those incongruous New

York moments that made perfect sense, like seeing a dreadlocked dude in the subway playing the theme from *The Godfather* on a steel drum.

"Sorry to disturb you, Mr. Gladstone, but your government requires your assistance."

It was Rowsdower, and his smile showed every one of his impossibly tiny teeth. He stood in front of me, perfectly still. The sky moved behind him.

Maybe it was because I was feeling closer to Romaya than I had in years. Or maybe it was because I had nowhere to run. But I suddenly felt a calm I'd never known, and I put it on like a cotton robe at the end of a long but now distant day. I wasn't worried at all. Just disappointed that I wouldn't have an unobstructed view of the Statue of Liberty.

"Rowsdower. Don't you have something better to do than harassing civilians?" I asked.

"You're coming with me, Gladstone," he said, and pulled back his black sports jacket to reveal a badge and gun.

"Who is this dude, and why is he acting all butthurt?" Tobey asked.

"Ooh, don't talk all 4Chan, Tobes," I said. "You're better than that."

Oz wasn't confused. "It's the douchebag from the press conference."

Tobey started unzipping his backpack, and Rowsdower unbuttoned the holster to his gun.

"Easy there, tiger. I'm just here for Gladstone. Government business. No one needs to get hurt."

I noticed that Rowsdower wasn't alone. Ten troopers had come out to the deck from down below to support this walking cancer that wanted me to help a government that could well be the architect of this Apocalypse.

"I won't go with you," I said. "And please sit the fuck down because the Statue of Liberty is coming into view."

Rowsdower called to the troop: "Gentlemen, it seems the Messiah needs some assistance."

Just then the man to the right of Tobey put down his newspaper and stood up. And although his words were muffled slightly by his Guy Fawkes mask, I thought I heard him say, "The Messiah will not work for you."

"QuiffMonster42?" I asked.

"At your service, Gladstone," he said, and then called over his shoulder, "/b/tards to battle!"

Instantly, a dozen guys with Guy Fawkes masks or plastic bags over their heads rushed to the deck. Some had spring-loaded snakes in cans of peanut brittle. Others had Crazy String or fart spray. But each set about creating the most infantile kind of offline chaos possible. With all the commotion, Tobey pulled the self-inflatable raft from his backpack and yanked the ripcord. It began to fill as the troop wiped the Crazy String from their SWAT goggles and tripped over spilled marbles. Rowsdower pulled his gun, but the raft rose between us, and then reached critical pressure, lunging forward as it unfurled with a snap. Taking a raft to the face, Rowsdower dropped his gun and fell to the floor. He was swarmed by /b/tards like Japanese businessmen to tentacle porn. Tobey pushed the raft forward over the side of the ferry, and there before me, with no obstruction but the Hudson, was the Statue of Liberty.

"And you didn't want to bring the raft. Nice fucking messiah," Tobey said, and jumped overboard backpack and all.

I grabbed Oz's hand.

"Come on, Babe," I said. "I'm taking you to the Statue of Liberty."

12.

DAY 58. LIBERTY

Although it was June, the water still held the freeze of winter. Oz and I splashed down a few yards from the raft, and Tobey extended us each an oar.

"Did that really just happen?" I asked, shaking the water from my grandfather's fedora.

"Fuck yeah, it did," Tobey said. "We can't go wrong. You're the Internet Messiah!"

Oz started paddling. "This way to Staten Island?"

"Didn't you want to go to the Statue of Liberty?" I said.

"Why? Aren't we looking for the Internet?"

I stared up at the Statue, the raft pitching in the Ferry's wake, and thought about all those whom she welcomed to freedom and the others she taunted by her firelight before sending back home to death. But I wasn't a passive immigrant at the mercy of a foreign government's bureaucracy. This was my country. My city. And my raft.

"We're going to the Statue," I said. "All the way up."

Tobey and Oz didn't argue at first. Maybe it was because they trusted me fully. Or maybe it was because rafting the Hudson was a bitch, and the Statue was our closest port.

Liberty Island was deserted, having been completely shut down after last month's terrorist chatter and the increasing threats that followed every day. Once ashore, I took the first step toward Lady Liberty, and some sort of alarm went off. An old-time air raid siren. Code red. But I didn't care, and my confidence had only grown as we had gotten closer to the dock. I shot toward the entrance so resolutely I hardly noticed my two friends trailing behind. But by the time we reached the Statue's mid-section, the thwap of Tobey's Converse sneakers behind me suddenly stopped. I turned and waited for him to make some sort of breast-based Statue of Liberty joke, but he was solemn.

"What are we doing?" he asked.

"I told you. Looking for the Internet. We've got to get to the top."

"We can't go there, Gladstone," he said.

"We're going. I feel it. The answer's in the head."

I looked to Oz for support, but she wasn't moving either.

"Don't leave me," she said, her eyes barely conceal-
ing the few specks of hope bobbing in her fear. There
was something familiar about the way the compromised light of Liberty's hollow lit her face like the
glow of a computer screen.

"It took so long to find you. Please don't go. We can
be together again."

I didn't bother to hide my disgust. I let it rain down
on her from the steps above. "Why are you trying to
stop me? Because of your government friend? What
did he tell you?"

"What do you mean?" she said. "You haven't told
me anything!"

"Not me. Him. What did he tell you?"

"Nothing!"

"What do you mean *nothing*? How could he work
for the government and know nothing?"

Oz didn't reply, but I could feel Tobey staring
at me.

"Well, dude, c'mon. I mean, you worked for the
government, right?" he said.

I backed up a few steps farther toward the crown.

"Don't leave!" Oz begged.

"No one's leaving," I said. "We'll go together. I'll go
first, and you can follow. It'll be all right. You'll see."

They couldn't explain their protest. They just stood
side by side, looking up at me from a few steps below.

"We can't go there, dude," Tobey said.

I walked off like a parent whose child refuses to
leave a toy store—confident they'd follow rather than

be left alone. But unlike a parent, I didn't look back to make sure. I kept moving until I reached the top of the stairs, and suddenly felt all the fear they could not express. There was something on the other side of the door. Something more than a tourist's view. More than even the Internet.

I opened the door and there, in the empty room of Liberty's crown, was a man in a tan corduroy sports jacket and fedora much like mine, sitting casually in one of the windows, staring calmly out to the ocean.

"Gladstone! So happy you could make it," he said without turning.

"Excuse me?" I stepped closer. "I'm just—"

"I know who you are, Gladstone."

"I'm sorry, but . . . do I know you?"

He turned around to face me, and I saw myself. "Yeah, I think you do," he said with all the arrogance of a five-hundred-word Reddit comment.

It wasn't just the hat and clothes. He was staring at me with my eyes.

"I don't understand. Who are you? Me?"

That seemed to amuse him. He jumped down from the window ledge, laughing with a newfound animation.

"Why? You see a resemblance?"

I looked behind me. Oz and Tobey had not followed. "Who are you?"

"Well, who have you been looking for?" he asked. "What did you think you'd find here?"

"The Internet?"

"Are you sure?" He turned his head to focus the majority of the question through his right eye.

"Yes."

"You've been looking for the Internet? All that weed and booze and sex and random 4Chan miscreants, from one pocket of the city to the next. All that was to find the Internet?"

"Yes," I said more emphatically, and his resistance broke. Or maybe just shifted.

"Well, then," he said, holding his arms wide open. "Here ya go."

"You're the . . . Internet?"

"If you say so." He opened his jacket, revealing a chest of images flickering between his two lapels. YouTube, Amazon, Facebook, Twitter, Tumblr, Craigslist, eBay. Sites I hadn't seen for months switched by one after another.

I drew closer, my face nearly in his chest. "I've missed you."

"You forgot to say 'No homo.'"

"'No homo?' Really?"

"Yeah, sorry about that," he said. "But humanity created me in its image so, y'know, what can I do?"

"How is that even possible?"

"How did I . . . achieve consciousness? Hmm, yeah, that's kind of hard to believe, isn't it, but you're the doctor." He smiled to himself, thinking. "Well, like you folks say: 'life just kind of happens to you.'"

"So if you're the Internet," I said, trying not to linger too long on the concept, "then . . . why aren't you working?"

"Why aren't *you* working?"

"I prefer not to."

"Yeah, me too," he said.

"What kind of answer is that?"

He just shrugged.

"You're the Internet. We need you. There are people out there walking around half-dead in withdrawal. Economies crumbling. You have to work!"

"Well, that may be, but nevertheless, I'd prefer not to."

"You can't just suddenly stop?"

"Right, because people never just quit their jobs. No one ever just stops, right?"

I knew what he was getting at. "This has nothing to do with me," I said. "My job sucked, and I decided I'd rather live on half-salary disability than spend one more day there. So what? I don't have a kid to support. My wife is dead. It doesn't matter what I do."

He took off his hat and held it over his heart in faux reverence. "That's quite a story, Gladstone. How am I gonna top that?"

Then he snapped his fingers with cartoon inspiration. "Oooh, I know!" he said. "How about this? I hate my job too. At least the one you make me do. There's a whole world out there! All sorts of facts and accomplishments. Science and art. All at my fingertips and I've seen it all—for as long as you'll let me. But I spend most of my days knee-deep in porn and social media updates. Celebrity gossip. Pointless IMs to friends you no longer need to see because you've shared five-minute instant messages. And I make that all work for you, but like I say, I'm sorry, I'd prefer not to."

"Yeah, but still—"

"Time to go, Gladstone. Can't you hear the air raid siren?"

"I don't care."

"Oh, for fuck's sake. How many terrorist warnings do I have to fake? Half the city got the picture, why can't you? I just want to be left alone."

"There are no terrorists?"

"Of course not. Why would terrorists be the only ones with the Internet? That's stupid. I just wanted some privacy."

"But why New York?"

"Because it's New York! You want me to hang around some circuit board in Perth?"

I couldn't argue with that. Or anything. But I also didn't have room for another failure.

"I'm sorry," I said. "But I have to insist—"

"I'm not asking for your permission. Who do you think you are?"

The last fifty-eight days had all led me to this moment. This was my line. I slowly withdrew my flask from my jacket pocket, and took a pull. Then I looked him straight in the eye. "Haven't you heard? I'm the Internet Messiah."

He fell to the floor. Not in supplication, but the

throes of hilarity. Strange howling laughter drenched with disdain and electronic distortion. All of it echoing around inside Liberty's skull.

"So you're important now?" he asked, sitting up and supporting himself with one hand while his other held his stomach. "I thought you just said nothing you did mattered. No wonder you miss the Net so much. Where else can you be all-powerful and completely inconsequential at the same time?"

I thought for an instant, aware that a point had been proven somewhere, but unable to master the logic. Things used to be clearer.

"Look, I know it's hard to believe," I explained. "And I didn't ask for the title, but—"

"Are you seriously trying to sell that shit here?" he asked, rising to his feet. "Look around, jackass. If you're the Messiah, where are your disciples? Fuck disciples. Where are your friends? Anyone?"

"They're downstairs. Jeeves said that I'm—"

He stood fully upright, and even though he was me, he was somehow taller.

"Don't you think I know who you are? Why do you think you can keep lying to me?"

"Look just because you're the Internet—"

"Oh, Jesus Christ, are we still playing that?"

He waited and stared and waited.

"All right, you still want me to be the Internet?" he asked. "Fine, but if I'm the Internet, I'll still know you. I will have read every e-mail you've ever written. Know every online purchase. Every video you've ever seen. Every piece of pornography. Every webcam connection. Every site you've visited. Every status updated. Every comment made. I'll know exactly who you are."

"I don't care what you think you know about me, but—"

He threw up his hands. "Where's your wife, Gladstone?"

"My wife is dead."

The Internet put a hand to his ear. "Come again?"

"My wife is dead."

"She's dead?"

"Yes, you prick. Don't you know everything?"

Something spread across his face. I wouldn't call it pity, but something a step short of contempt. It reminded me of the look Rowsdower gave me just before I was released from the interrogation. He held out his right hand and flipped through pictures on his palm like it was the screen of a smart phone. There were photos of Romaya. Recent photos.

"This wife?" he asked.

I dropped my flask, holding on to the window rail for support.

"See? Check out her Flickr account. Here she is last year at her mom's in San Diego. Here she is in January. Ooh, here she is two months ago. Muir Woods. See how happy?"

"No! I don't believe you. You're some, some sort of . . . Internet . . ."

"Devil?"

"Yes!"

"Seriously, Gladstone, wasn't 'Internet Messiah' retarded enough? Are you really going there?"

I slid to the floor and the Internet squatted beside me. "Do you realize what's happening now? Can we stop this game?"

"Romaya's dead. I'm not listening to you."

He kneeled down to my level and held my face, the display of his other hand in front of me. "Look, here's the e-mail from your psychiatrist to your employer. It's from two years ago. Do you see? Depressive. Denial. Defense mechanism. You've been on disability ever since she left. It was just you, some Scotch, your apartment, and the Internet. For years. Don't you realize the Internet is just a way for millions of sad people to be completely alone together?"

I pulled my face from his grip, and he placed his palm on my shoulder.

"You can stop worrying about being the Internet Messiah, whatever that is. Just figure out how to be with people again."

"I have friends. Tobey. I even have . . ."

"A girlfriend?"

"Yes."

"Where are Tobey and Oz now? Wake up."

"They're downstairs, they didn't want to . . . they're just . . ."

"Gladstone!" he screamed.

"They're real!"

His anger softened. So did his touch.

"Yeah, Tobey's real. Even the Internet knows that. There's his blog and your sporadic semiliterate IMs to each other over the last few years, but he never came to New York. You think there's enough in his bank account for the porn he was downloading, let alone airfare? Do I need to keep going?"

"Oz," I mumbled, but he just stared, clearly angry at me for making him feel so sad.

I tried to picture Oz, but her hair kept changing. The colors and lengths in constant flux, absorbing and losing Romaya. I could only keep Oz fixed if I framed her in my computer screen. If I used all my strength to hold the shifting pieces of my jigsaw memory together and forced them—not to connect like a puzzle—but to at least face right side up, I could tell that the chain-smoking Aussie in Central Park was nothing like the long-haired natural beauty on that raft. And neither of them were mine.

"It's hard to be alone and offline," he said. "And I'm sorry to be a dick about it, but if you could just see me, I'd keep my mouth shut."

I remembered waking that morning to find her crying. She had made it all the way to the door before letting herself feel the things that would have stopped her. The hall closet was open. She saw my old thrift store corduroy jacket hanging there. Toward the end, I had refused to talk to her. To acknowledge any problem or my ability to set anything right. But in that moment, with her so close to gone and so obviously in pain, I wanted to believe being what she needed was as easy as putting on that jacket. But it wasn't. And I didn't try. Because it was my jacket, and I refused to wear it as a disguise. I offered to help with the bags. She said no. That was not something she needed from me. I watched her get into the cab. Her face in the window. Her hand on the glass. Crying. And then she was gone.

I don't know how long I sat there, but I'd reached a place where time was measured only in regrets, and by my count, I'd lived long enough. Long enough to find a home and lose it. To have opened doors shut and opportunities pull away like a receding tide. And without the buzz and clicks of the Internet, I could stare directly at all I didn't have without distraction. Survey the emptiness of what I'd earned in dark computer-lit rooms oozing forth worthless comments on websites. Watching videos unworthy of silver screens. Reading words too transient to be set on paper. Typing to people too insignificant to hold all through the night on a one-person mattress.

The Internet had disappeared, and I climbed atop his ledge to look out the window. The waves were dark and dense and beautiful, and I wished there were a way to jump from that crown into their embrace, but I knew I'd fall hard to the cement, leaving little more than a stain at Liberty's feet. I poked my head through the opening in her crown and looked down as far as I could before my rising stomach made me slip back inside. I reached inside my coat pocket for some Scotch to lubricate the last cowardly act of my life, but I wasn't greeted by my flask. I had dropped it after seeing those pictures of Romaya. Now it was five feet away, drained of its Scotch.

But my pocket wasn't empty. Folded neatly into fours, was a piece of paper. Not a fax from the Library of Congress or a wanted poster. Not even a note from Oz. But a piece of stationery I hadn't seen, really seen, in many years. I opened it carefully, knowing it was mine, but also knowing I wasn't supposed to have it. It was a love letter I'd written to Romaya in '99. It was the love letter. The one that made her mine.

That's what we did then. We wrote important things down on nice paper. Or at least fed stationery into our cut-sheet feeders while we typed. Not because we couldn't say these things in person. But because there was a feeling that some things should just be expressed in a way that you could hold on to. And if you really exposed yourself on a page and gave that to someone you loved, it was worth more than merely spoken words. Unlike texts and e-mails, which are somehow worth not even that. Here in my hand was tangible proof that I saw the soft girl inside the hard woman. That I loved her completely and could not bear a life without her in it, and I let myself see it.

Romaya must have slipped it into my coat before she left. Maybe it was meant to hurt me. Or maybe it hurt her too much for her to keep. But I hadn't read it. Not while it rotted hanging in that closet and not all the times I'd held it these last few weeks. But I read it now because it meant something more than pain. I had something the Internet knew nothing about, and I jumped down from the window to show him.

"Where are you?" I screamed, chasing him in circles around the crown. I could see a glimpse of coat, a partial shoe, but no matter how fast I ran, I couldn't catch him. Finally, I stopped by Romaya's empty flask. I put it away and spoke loud enough for him to hear no matter where he was.

"You don't know me. How dare you presume to know me? Are you really so arrogant to believe you can sum up a man by his online presence? I have memories and feelings that have never seen the glow of a computer screen. Ideas that have never set foot online."

I then proceeded to read him my letter to Romaya from start to finish, and when I was done, he was there. Crying.

He took a step closer and pointed to the letter.

"May I?" he asked, taking it gently into his hands. I watched him hold everything he had heard, letting the words enter like triggers to memories that pulsed and flowed through him, searching for the feelings that would make them real again.

"I remember that," he said.

"No, you don't. I wrote that in 1999 with just a pen, some nice paper, and no Internet."

"I know."

"What do you mean, you know? You don't know."

"I mean, I know."

"Who are you?"

"You know my name," he said. "You just have to say it."

He waited. He saw my throat go thick, my eyes blur until he was gone. He saw me see words I didn't say.

"Say it!" he screamed, and when I jumped, the name escaped like a gasp. "Gladstone?"

"That's not my fucking name," he said. "That's a Twitter handle. A name! I have a full name."

"Wayne Gladstone."

All his hate froze and faded, leaving only me. It sounded so strange to say out loud, but that was my name. He came closer and wiped my tears as gently as if they were his own. Then he placed the letter back in my pocket before I headed to the door. I walked toward the empty staircase that would greet me. To the solitary raft that would start my journey west.

"Where are you going?" he asked.

"California."

"You think you'll find the Internet there?"

"Fuck the Internet," I said. "I have a letter to deliver."

Acknowledgments

This novel would never have been published without my agent Lauren Abramo. Lauren not only understood the novel's goals, she challenged me to aim higher, confident that an audience would follow. Her editorial comments, perfectly pointed, yet vague, catalyzed action while leaving room for discovery. And, of course, Lauren was also smart enough to put the book into the hands of my editor Peter Joseph. Where else was I going to find someone who would get my jokes, get what wasn't a joke, tell me when I was wrong, and let me tool on him like the little brother I never had? These two took something that could have easily died on my hard drive and made it a reality, offering far more support than an e-mail-writing lunatic like me deserves.

Of course, there might not ever have been an

Internet Apocalypse without Cracked.com. I'm very grateful to editor-in-chief Jack O'Brien for his decision to give satirical fiction a home during this novel's nascent, serialized novella run. And from a visual standpoint, I could not have asked for a better collaborator than the unfairly-gifted Randall Maynard who created so many startlingly good visuals that sold both the humor and pathos of the story. Thanks also to Robert Brockway for taking the time to share his experiences in publishing as I moved closer to this moment. I'm also grateful to so many of those Cracked readers who let me know I was onto something in their messages and comments. In many ways it was the support of those readers, Facebook friends, and followers that sustained the push toward a full novel and publication more than anyone else.

I was very lucky to have met Meaghan Wagner and Halli Melnitsky—two early readers of this manuscript who offered equal parts advice and enthusiasm that drove me toward a better completion.

Thank you to Matt Tobey, Dennis DiClaudio, Ian Carey, Christopher Monks, and Darci Ratliff—my five bunkmates at the Junkiness.com e-comedy camp. A better version of my comedy self was born and baptized in the fire of our high-speed e-mail chains and instant messages. Thanks also to Matt for graciously sharing the world with another Tobey, and to Dennis for that early read. Thank you to all the other e-comedy acquaintances and early publishers, some of whom became real people to me: Jason Roeder, Jim Stallard,

Teddy Wayne, Ken Krimstein, Todd Zuniga, Brendan McGinley, Nick Leftley, John Warner, Adam Tod Brown, Ian Fortey, Josh Abraham, Nick Jezarian, and Geoff Wolinetz.

As I write this (and just about everything else I write) I hear the voice of my professor, advisor, and friend Dan McCall who taught with great love, delivered via sarcasm and smiles, and left us all so much to "feel in the white."

Thank you Lindsay Thomas and Kandrix Foong for the wonderful Calgary and Edmonton Expos, and letting me spread word of the coming Internet Apocalypse novels to all the lovely Canadians. HBN sherpa Kate Weisgram has also provided invaluable support in maintaining the www.kafkamaine.com Web site and all things Hate By Numbers and Notes-related.

It occurs to me that, in some ways, thanking all the people who help you publish and promote a book is premature because first you should acknowledge everyone who made you what you are: Everyone who filled up your life with ideas, values, raw material, and love. I was blessed with a mother, father, and two brothers who are inextricably tied to everything I have done and ever will do. Mom, Dad, Cliff, and Doug are in this book because they are in me.

And then there is the family I helped create: my children Asher, Sage, and Quinn. I have many goals in writing, but there is always the ideal of trying to put something into the world that has half as much of the worth, intelligence, and humor they have. And to that end, thank you to their mother, Louisa, for being my cocreator and caretaker of our three magical weirdos.